More praise for

The Seven Stages of Anger
AND OTHER STORIES

"Wendy J. Fox's prose is strong and fragile at the same time. As she explores in these stories the hairline fractures in our relationships with life, ourselves and each other, you can't help but hold your breath for the big break you know is coming. The eggshells of everything? Fox owns the category."

— Anastasia Ashman
editor of *Tales From The Expat Harem*

"Wendy J. Fox's stories capture a world of grit, sunlight, heat, love and lust—a fully Western world as spare, arresting and luminous in its details as the prose she uses to describe it. Populated with memorable, deadpan characters—wry, likable for their hidden strengths and never entirely unhopeful despite whatever hard luck they face—her stories often spin on metaphors so richly extended that their complexity takes on a life and force of its own. The end result is a vision as sharp, imaginative, full of longing and illuminated in poetry as any I've recently read. A fantastic debut and great new voice on the scene!"

— Gregory Spatz
author of *Half as Happy*

THE SEVEN STAGES OF ANGER

The Seven Stages of Anger
AND OTHER STORIES

Winner of the Press 53 Award for Short Fiction

WENDY J. FOX

Press 53
Winston-Salem

Press 53, LLC
PO Box 30314
Winston-Salem, NC 27130

First Edition

THE SEVEN STAGES OF ANGER AND OTHER STORIES
Winner of the 2014 Press 53 Award for Short Fiction

Cover design by Kevin Morgan Watson

Cover art, "Seattle Softly Awakens" Copyright © 2014
by Stacy Ann Young, used by permission of the artist.

Printed on acid-free paper
ISBN 978-1-941209-07-3

To My Parents, Audrey & Wayne

ACKNOWLEDGMENTS

The author gratefully acknowledges the editors of the publications where the following stories first appeared.

"Apricots" appeared as "The Fire Time" in *The Pisgah Review*, Summer 2008.

"The Car" appeared in *10,000 Tons of Black Ink*, Fall 2012.

"Fauntleroy" appeared in *Washington Square Review*, Issue 26, Summer/Fall 2010.

"The House" appeared in *PMS poemmemoirstory*, 2010, Issue 11.

"Ten Penny" appeared in *The Pinch*, Volume 28, Issue 2, Fall 2008.

"The Seven Stages of Anger" appeared in *The Madison Review*, Fall 2008.

"There and Back" appeared in *The Broome Review*, Spring 2011.

"Zinc" appeared in *The Puritan*, Spring 2012.

The Seven Stages of Anger

AND OTHER STORIES

Apricots

As children growing up in the eastern Washington desert, the dry side of the Cascades, we learned to speak of rain the way we spoke of the dead: with reverence, with longing, without hope of return. We lived in the country, and I mean all of us. Everyone we knew in the world. We were a pack of half a dozen kids, I the only girl, none of us past pre-teen. Even when we were small, we had to do things like pick rocks, piling up the pebbles and larger hunks of shale and granite into heaps around the perimeter of the gardens, where there would be a thicket of marigolds—bright yellow and orange ruffles planted because the stink kept the insects down.

When our parents would take out their machines, tractors and rototillers, they would deftly skirt these pyramids, leaving a band of sage and knapweed like a moat circling the tiers of stone that had become our crypts for grasshoppers and field mice and refuse from illicit picnics we'd had with vegetables and jam stolen from the root cellars, and the occasional half-smoked cigarette buried with Kerr lids and carrot tops.

But, if we weren't doing our chores or sneaking or at the neighbors', we spent time out on the low, brown hillsides, trudging among the trees turned brittle and along the dirt cow paths. Up in the land behind our respective homes, there were spindly timbers and scrub and dried lichens on the exposed rock. We would find a walking stick and get to it.

The year of the fire, it had not rained for months. We lived for days with the sun obscured by atmospheric dust, with the air choked with pollen. Maybe it was a decade with no rain; no one knew. I remember the sizzle of everything, the way my hair broke off at the ends, the static electricity everywhere. My parents' well was failing. Our yard was long gone, and the lilac bush slumped against the side of the house, blooms dropped and drying around the base. The strawberry beds and raspberries were paper. We had a plot of wilty potatoes, a cherry tree, and brittle greens, though nearby our southern neighbor's heat-loving wheat fields glowed as gold as a pharaoh's polished tomb. The fields were on a plateau, where the land was mostly flat and open, but there were a few pines poking out through the yellow stalks or fallow dirt. Shade and topsoil were precious, and the farmer had not wanted to cut the trees or destroy the root systems that held the ground in place when the wind blew, even if it meant extra turns on the combine.

We spent a great deal of time concerned with food. My family cleaned meat and honey, and we would trade for milk, for cheese. There was an extractor for the honey—a galvanized barrel maybe four feet tall, with screens mounted around an axle that the combs from the beehives would slip between. Off the side hung a crank and I could turn it if someone would get it started for me. The honey splattered out of the matrix of wax and was collected from a spigot at the bottom, amber draining in the glass gallon jars we also used for milk jugs. We did this in my father's shop, surrounded by the tools and packets of grease and planks of woods and bundles of wire he'd collected over a lifetime.

In season, he would hang a beef or pork or venison from the winch that was mounted in the rafters. Before he took up bow hunting, he made his own bullets, melting down wheel weights to smelt lead into shot for the muzzleloader or carefully filling shells with gunpowder and saltpeter. The winch had a big hook attached to a chain, and it wasn't initially there to butcher—he had installed it so he could pull an engine. If there was nothing up, my brother and I and sometimes the other kids would yank the pulley chain until the hook was a good height and swing back and forth on it, dangling there between the arc welder and the wood lathe. But when there was an animal up, I was set up with a bench and a low table and two stainless steel bowls. One bowl held scraps and one held the meat after it was ground, and it was my job to run these scraps through the electric grinder, painted green and on indefinite loan from Grandpa.

Every once in awhile, the grinder would clog, and then I was to run a piece of hard fat through it, and I enjoyed the sound it made as it churned through—almost like popcorn popping. Mostly, though, I did not like these days. The sticky smells, the glassy eyes of a deer (my father, for years, would toss the buck horns on top of the woodshed, and there they stayed, pointed bone, until, fearful of fire, he moved the wood away from the house and tore down the shed). Or the beef hide, rotting, down on the burn pile: I saw early on that even a fast death could feel very slow, how we turn cold easily, and how the blood of different beasts looks the same where it pools around the exit wound, sinks into the ground, and disappears.

The night the fire started, the sky had cleared. It was hot. If I stayed perfectly still, I was almost comfortable, but the minute I moved, the heat would swirl around me like when I ran bathwater with too much red and not enough blue. I remember how clearly I had wanted night to come and along with it the promise of at least a minute of cool, but instead, the sky opened, electric. Lightning hit the hillsides with the sound and force of an animal coming down: the crack of a shot, smoke gathering, the thud of something living going hard to the ground.

My mother let me stay up past midnight to watch the hillside blaze.

Even from miles off, I heard trees exploding, a hundred years of pine, gone. I don't know how I felt besides in awe of the ignition or if I had a sense of the way the flame was moving.

Days passed as our fathers scratched at the dirt with their axes, trying to loosen enough earth to suffocate the flames, with little success. Then the families on our rural mountainside tried a controlled back-burn of their own land and barns before the natural fire got there—an attempt to leave no fuel so they could at least save the houses. The roads closed. The gardens singed. Our mothers cooked whatever they could find to feed their lovers and husbands, grown and half-grown sons. When the already sporadic electricity quit, they made cauldrons of meat. In my lifetime, I couldn't count the number of chickens I'd seen my mother behead, picking them up by their legs and flinging them onto a round of wood, lopping off at the neck, and in the heat with no ice and the deep freeze gone, a year's worth of butchering began to turn.

After more days passed, the state finally arrived, and they decided to evacuate the children and anyone else who would go to the non-denominational church in town. On this day, we saw an amazing thing: a helicopter dumped a trough of blood-red fire retardant across the hills and then landed in the fields. Then we were all in the back of a silver van with heart-shaped windows. I saw between other kids in our getaway vehicle, little people with sunflower hair and eggplant eyes, and I prayed nothing would ever separate us, ever. More helicopters came. We were children who played war and who would sever the heads off snakes with a shovel or a sharp rock, but we had never seen anything like these *choppers,* as we so expertly called them. The helicopters bombed the fire with water and chemical to make a portal along the gravel roads, and we sped through in the silver van, and we watched another huge machine touch down among the charred alfalfa and the ruined wheat.

When we made it to the church, we discovered our fire had become an event. It was larger than we had known—the flames curling around the back side of the hills and into some of the other enclaves that flanked the town. And we heard two of the town men discussing it. We heard them talking about what kind of people lived there, on our mountain, how we were just *hill people* anyway, how we couldn't have much worth saving. We had barely, some of us, started our years of education then, and we knew some people bought most of their food at the store and wore clothes other than hand-me-downs. As an odd job, my father even drove some of us to school, in a four-wheel drive panel van with SCHOOL DISTRICT 404 stamped on the side. I think we had known for a long time that we were different, we just didn't know how much it mattered.

My parents kept their home, their barn, the shop and the cellar.

Their upper tract burned, but ultimately, we were out little. Even our well came back and came back clean. I had a pony—not a fancy ribbon in the hair type, but a work pony with lower GI distress—who farted constantly when he walked, and he got a stick in his eye, but one of my father's friends extracted it. Some of us, though, lost nearly everything. All that was left by one rock outcropping where one of our families had built a home was a blackened concrete slab. The chicken coop stood, though even the chickens, who'd been let out to fend for themselves, were ash.

Years later, two of us, grown and back for some holiday, hiked back there on the trails we had traveled as children, with our adult shoes too wide for the paths, and from there we opened that chicken coop door, which came unstuck with a sound like cartilage separating from bone. Inside there was nothing much: the molting of long-dead birds and a smell from a time when we sat in a church we were not members of and cried so hard we choked.

I remembered how I cleaned one of the Sunday school rooms, even putting all the chairs up on the tables so I could crawl along the floor and pick the scraps out of the carpet, and then two of the boys came behind me and knocked it all down, upturned the bins of broken crayons and the tubes of glue I had sorted, and shredded the picture books. Maybe they already knew, with a certainty I still cannot match, how the fire would change us.

Before the ground even cooled most of the families left the hillside. Some moved to houses in town, and thus began our parting. I stayed on and learned to gather the morel mushrooms and the stands of fireweed that had grown in the years following the torching of a forest. My family harvested the scorched pine and tamarack and used what was left of it in the woodstoves through the deep winters. We took only the trees that were dead, and every year, during the summer and the fall when we'd go cutting, we'd be dusted in charcoal again, the burnt bark crumbling in our hands.

I still fear electrical storms and a spark in a dry place. I still remember the way the sky darkened and the smoke bloodshot our eyes. I still remember the ethylene stink of crackling-dry air, and I remember how, the day we visited and we pried loose the seal on the chicken coop door, with the bare rock around us, how I hoped, liked I hoped for rain that summer, and I hope even now, that in some of those sealed-up, untouched places, there could be a way back to a place before the fire, that split our clan as easily as we used to open apricots with our fingers.

I picture us there, after scrambling up a rock pile or in the crook of a tree that's now fallen, flush with having stolen or just the promise of sweet, dividing the bisected halves, swallowing the fruit and spitting the center into the dirt. Maybe some of these pits will have cleaved and rooted; even a new shoot can withstand ferocious heat.

Even if, those years ago, we found nothing behind the chicken coop door, I still comb the ground for green.

Fauntleroy

Once, I lived with my lover, a country boy, who could have been one of my brothers. We liked to think we weren't really hilljacks (this was my word for it) anymore, since we'd gone off to college in Seattle and stayed in the city. But the thing about country people is, they can move to a new geography, be thrust into the routines that seem normal for the rest of the world, but they still have the dirt in them. They still feel the kickback of a rifle on their shoulder, they still expect trouble. And because they look for it, they find it.

My lover—the one I did not marry, that I could not—was a year younger than me, so I'd left our small hometown before he did. At first, we'd moved fairly anonymously through our shared university campus. Then, through a drizzle, I saw him and I thought, *I know you.* It was more than simple recognition. I'd grown up with this boy. He'd pissed in streams with my brothers, our parents were friends, and we'd spent days together as children plotting against the tyranny of adults. And for the next several years, I spotted him almost every day, but I ignored him because he was proof of the place I'd left. I was working hard to build a different kind of life.

One day, in a coffee shop off campus, just as my graduation neared, he stopped me. He said he only wanted to say hello. He said, *It has been hard for me here. I thought maybe we could talk.*

Sometimes when someone reaches for you, you reach back.

I have a memory of me young, my brothers and me, when we were just a girl and some boys in eastern Washington, all piled onto my parents' brown sofa. It was summer and I was in a typical summer dress, frayed hem, the fabric itself a non-color from being washed and worn and worn more than it was washed.

I was just on the cusp of adolescence, and maybe I hadn't really learned yet what people can do to other people, though even at a young age, country children know something of the ugliness of adults. Country children are not kind. They live close to animals and the dirt, and they turn the idyllic forests and fields into battlegrounds. They learn to handle weapons, to slaughter fowl and four-leggeds. They are accustomed to hides and gasoline, and being out in all kinds of weather. And they also learn to protect themselves, because they have eaten their pet piglets, watched their seedlings die, chopped the heads off of snakes with the barn shovels, and they have not learned to believe that they are any different, any less immune to brutality.

This, though, was not one of those violent times. My brothers, David at the foot of the couch and Glen, the youngest, on the cushions by me, had been perfectly quiet for several minutes, and so had I.

Often I came back to us like this, our six bare, dirty feet and unwashed hands, our shiny eyes, our lips pressed closed. It was rare that our bodies were so close, rare that we as a group resembled anything like still. Usually we were covered in mud and tumbling into or out of something.

We were facing the wall. Our parents had a little television, but it wasn't on, and we didn't notice. It was not quite stinking hot yet, but it would be soon, and we seemed to have promptly forgotten what we came for.

I remember I felt like inertia was the thing I was made of, instead of my usual: all raging, tender guts.

I wanted to fold into David; he was only two years younger than me, but I already felt us pulling apart, and I wanted to haul Glen into my lap, even though at six he was too old for it. Both of them, as children, were as blond as wheat; we all were sunburned.

And then, more than closeness, I wanted deep promises from them. I wanted to hear Glen, who was as menacing as soap, say something fierce or wicked; I wanted Davey to join him, and I wanted them to swear their allegiances to each other and then, finally, to me. I thought, *They are my brothers and I love them,* and I wanted proof.

It passed, though. The screen door slammed in the wind or maybe one of them burped, and we all remembered we had been promised popsicles—which to us were generally just ice cubes— or that we had a captured grasshopper waiting in a glass jar to have her legs ripped off or that we were in a fight, and we got up and went back to our day.

Years later, I was the first-generation college student visiting home after a successful year at university, and Davey had taken the GED to get out of high school a year early. He was studying for his welding certificate at a technical college, and I saw suddenly how his hair had gone brown, how his face became rough in the afternoon, how his hands, already, had the thick, broken skin of a man who works with them. Glen was still small to me; he had become slim and inward and, like his brother, a brunet. He mostly stayed in his room and listened to his albums. For months.

I didn't know what had happened to them, my boys. It was more than growing up. It was absence. I realized I didn't have anything to say to them, that I had rarely thought of them in the past year, that I had come to my parents' home mostly out of a habit I was trying to break.

This is what distance does.

Barely a decade later, we three live in three places so different that we don't experience the same seasons, and when we look at the sky, our horizons would not be recognizable to one of the others.

Daniel courted me in a way that seemed appropriate and familiar. A friend of his parents' who lived in town had given him a busted-up pickup and we drove out to the gray northern Pacific beaches and said nothing for a long time while collecting broken sand dollars. We rode the ferries out to the islands, had a coffee, and came back. Once we took the train to Portland. We'd grown up always wanting to disappear from where we were, and it was hard to shake the habits of leaving.

He was thin and soft, and like a bridge between one world and the next.

By the time we moved in to a house on Fauntleroy together, I thought I was a tasseographer of his body.

I watched him.

He came home one day with a bruise on his upper thigh, and the more it came out, the more it looked like the shape of a mouth instead of a run-in with the corner of a table like he'd said. I wondered who had bit him so hard he couldn't tell me; I wondered who had tried to take him whole in her mouth. I knew from my readings the other marks of his body—the crescent scar above his left eye (and the similar one above my right), the raspberry on his shoulder from being hit very, very hard by a baseball decades ago (the summer he was fourteen), and one long, permanent scratch down his index finger (his otherwise perfect hands).

This was around the time I was having problems at my job. I had also discovered psychiatry. Sometimes I'd take twice my usual Zoloft before I went to work just so I could be serotonin-stoned because it gave the morning a thick, underwater feeling that I liked. My employer, a small contractor, was close to where we lived. I did permitting and paperwork, mostly, which I was very good at, when I tried.

Anyway, the drugs, if I took extra, would wrench my gut and occasionally—before I got a tolerance going—I'd throw up and my boss would let me go home. If I'd driven the truck, it took me a whole three minutes to get back to our house; if I'd walked, maybe more like fifteen.

I really did do good work when I paid attention, but considering how much time I'd taken to spending in the bathroom, my employer was unhappy with me, and while I knew it, I couldn't do anything about it because of the trouble that had started with Daniel.

By the time all this was happening, we found out I was pregnant, and our shared childhood of me—because I was the older one—forcing him to play house looked like it might come true. I should say when *he* found out I was pregnant, because I knew from day one. I've heard it is like that sometimes. He was already asking me questions because he'd bring me a beer and I couldn't finish it. Just physically couldn't.

When I bought the box of tests, there were two inside, individually wrapped. The first was a dud. No response. I had to wait another hour before I could pee again, and the feeling was pretty clear—I was being stalled. I didn't need to wait and see the + poking through the plastic window on the white plastic stick, but it worked all right for me as a confirmation, and a way to tell him. I dropped the test on the kitchen table, and then he said I had to stop taking the Zoloft, but I didn't.

And, I didn't ask Daniel about the bruise, though I wanted to. I wanted to shake the words out of him and have them spit into my hand like a set of milk teeth. I remember one night, when it had turned green before it faded out, I made a batch of corn bread and brought it to him with butter while he read in the living room. He wanted to know why I'd baked it, but I couldn't say why, except that I had a craving. So maybe he got his bruise like that—a little impulse made real. We sat on the sofa and had our respective squares and he said, *This is really good*, and I said, *Thanks*, and that was all; we ate in the half dark, our teeth cutting all the way through.

It was a long way for us to land in Seattle, together, where the air was damp like a body. There was mold growing around the windows of our house, but we didn't mind. Sometimes we'd stand out in the perpetual rain, wet up to the shins in our tall, never-mowed grass, and tip our heads back to the sky. Nothing could burn us in that town, and for the two of us, who held the same dark scars of perpetual summer forest fires, this was a blessing. We were soaked and we stayed soaked.

When I think about it now, though, I think maybe he wasn't so grateful for all that water we were surrounded by, water from the west, water from the ground, water from the sky.

After the corn bread day, everything in the house started dying. My houseplants drooped. Fruit spoiled. The yard smelled like yeast. Especially if I was alone, I'd find smells lurking all over. I remembered once in my family home, a winter when the owls had gotten bold and carried off all of our cats, and finally, the mice began to take over our house. My father, if he found one, would catch it in a jar and throw it into the woodstove. He was not unkind to animals as a general rule but had a deep vendetta toward rodents and starlings. Finally, we had to put out poison, which worked much better than Dad's method. Our mice filled their guts and then slunk off into the walls to die. The smell of fur and bellies eaten from the inside out hung inside for a good week.

With Daniel and I—or maybe just me—it was just a rotten, unplaceable stink. Maybe it was the pregnancy, but I had clods of hair coming out and plugging the drain. There was a black spot on the gum above my right incisor.

I guess I was sick as those mice then. Daniel said I had taken to talking in my sleep; I did not know if it was true, but I did know that my dreams were restless and for the first time in many years I could not remember them. I knew that I would wake and be startled or disoriented and he would say, *I'm here*, and though I pushed my body into his, I wasn't always so sure he was what I needed.

I had a desperate feeling about him—that I wanted him and wanted him gone at the same time. That is a feeling something like fear. It is a feeling like a moth must feel, driven to chew her way out of the cocoon, terrified at what she might find.

What I mean is I was open to the possibility of disaster, to the trouble we were so used to.

I don't like to admit how suspicious I was. I was suspicious of everything, not only of Daniel, though I was preoccupied with the bruise. It was real, by all definitions: I could see it, I could feel it raised from his skin; I know the taste would have been bitter in my mouth.

I liked to say that I had known him since he was born. Probably this is true. Probably when I was screaming at eleven months old and he was screaming, even newer to the world, I knew him. Our mothers, if not fast friends, were neighbors. One night, in the Fauntleroy house, Daniel kicked open one of the low cabinet doors in the kitchen and hiked his leg up to rest his foot on the top near the hinge, I saw that in us, our history. He'd let his hair go wild. I said he looked like Walt Whitman. He played songs on his guitar and then, after, counted out the timing to help me understand how he'd made them.

Another thing that was a problem was in the evening I would start crying. I said I couldn't stop crying, but I didn't *want* to stop. When I cried, he'd hold onto me like he craved every slope of my skin, not like I was just the default body around the house.

Then the grass went dormant and the roses dried up. Not that we'd ever taken care of the roses. And, I had always loved how the morning glories snaked through our yard, a takeover done all in white, but then our landlord came and hacked at what was left of the under-tended beds around the house. Mostly, after the roses keeled over and the blooming weeds were ripped out, all she had left to do was pull mint that had gone infestive and poke at some stubby rhododendrons.

Still, I was angry at the pile of vine composting over by the recycling. We lived there and we paid for it and it seemed like if I liked the yard to be more of a thicket I could have it that way. Daniel said that was not really the way it worked.

I guess I didn't have a lot of sympathy for him, sometimes. Did he think I thought his bruise was only a smear of charcoal? We didn't use wood-burning stoves anymore. I thought he was leaving me. I *knew* he was leaving me and I was enraged. The morning glories were nothing. What did we do then. We'd share some poems, swap a song or two, and then hunker down on the couch with our corn bread. Chewing.

All of which is to say, I blame the pregnancy and I blame our shared memories, but neither of us is absolved. There is not enough water in this world for our ablutions. I read once that the Koran says if there's no water around it's okay to use dirt or sand as long as the body parts get done in the right order. The point is that people try. So okay. Maybe we weren't trying. I felt pretty tried out, actually.

I suppose he and I had grown up doing enough farming that we should have expected the weather would turn on us. The rain helped him find the mouth that bit the bruise into his leg; the rain licked me between my thighs and found my belly. The rain made my head mushy.

In the Fauntleroy house, it was like a thousand years had passed. Maybe we were fated. I think sometimes I did feel more like his sister than his lover. When we met again, we were reluctant to tell our families or anyone we knew from home. But why else would he have found me, if not to take our lives back from the ash of that place.

But then again, I was pregnant and he was bitten. Neither one of us was exactly at our best. Also, we were having too many Very Long Talks. I'd been fired by that time and Daniel was between jobs, so we had time for it. Mostly he was distressed and scared about what was happening in my body. Mostly I was distressed and scared about what I could see on his.

Then one day, I put on the kettle to make tea and forgot about it. I'd taken the whistler out of the spout because I didn't like the screech. Yes, it was caffeinated, and I wasn't supposed to be having caffeine, but the tea soothed me, and I saved the bags for my eyes, which were swollen a lot. It was awhile before we smelled it, the scorch of metal on metal. We both went running for the kitchen. When I lifted the kettle off the burner, he said, *Careful*, and he said it so softly I nearly dropped the pot—it was startling to hear his whisper.

Then I didn't know what to think, because it seemed like a little accident like forgetting the tea water caused so much to turn. Because after that I wasn't actually pregnant anymore. There wasn't a lot of blood or anything like that, but I think whoever was in there decided to get us on the next round. I did feel like one of those small, drafty houses from our childhood after that. I did feel like I was back in the moo-dust landscape we used to live in. I did smell sage constantly, though it certainly didn't grow close to the Fauntleroy house. I did realize that combustion isn't so simple as I'd thought—he and I might have landed in a wet clime, but there are still all kinds of smolder. Think of how a stack of wet rags or pile of compost might ignite: slowly, and without the drama of a match, of gasoline, of the sky's electricity. It's almost worse.

So there we were. Fire makes some soft things, like wood, hard, or the heat causes little fissures to explode. I guess it works that way on insides, because we split then. I hadn't wanted to think that he was just hanging around because he'd accidentally knocked me up, but there I had it.

How terrified I was, how sad. When we packed up our things it was like there was nothing left of the time we'd spent in the house. I was scared to touch him, as much as I wanted to feel his skin. I asked him if he was going off to his lover, the one who had bruised him. He was hauling something and he said, *Stop looking at me like that, don't look at me,* so I did. I stopped.

I moved into a house with some friends from college, and I spent a lot of time on the porch, in the rain. I would think, *This is what it's like to be stuck.* I would think, *This is exactly what I was trying to avoid.* I would miss Daniel. Sometimes I would make a batch of corn bread and throw it out. I would sit out on the porch so I wouldn't have to smell it. My roommates left me alone.

From my seat outside, I would watch the cars go by, the Nissans and Fords and Volkswagens. I was always good at recognizing the make or model of a car, but the years eluded me. Then on a larger scale—I could not have said what part of time I fit into.

What I was experiencing was a lack of concentration.

What I was experiencing was not an experience at all, but a state.

What I was experiencing was the way the things that aren't really things at all, like light, attach to the body and make it glow. I would close my eyes and see someone grinding grain on a grist wheel, or one dirty-faced boy snapping his stick at a herd of calves, all outlined like an after-image of staring at the sun.

And I would see Daniel, from the time we were children, from the time when my brothers and I still knew each other, from the time when we believed that leaving the farmlands would erase them. I heard that he had moved back home, and though I wanted to follow him there, I resisted it. I felt a little tougher, a little more cactus, a little less moss. But Daniel's skin—I could see his skin clearly, as impeccably smooth as water. And, as water, maybe there would be movement underneath, or maybe a group of thrashing kids would wreck the plane with a cascade of rocks. I started to believe I was wrong about the bruise, because no matter what happened, no matter how I could see him ripple to the touch or his surface scar briefly, he would go back to perfect every time.

Zinc

When our daughter was three, I told my husband, Julian, that I was leaving.

"Why?" he asked. "I didn't see this."

It was harder to explain than I expected. The ideas were there, but I had a hard time getting the words out of my mouth.

"I need to make a change," I said, frustrated at how this sounded, like the sound of a spoon against a pan: hollow, metallic.

"Could we try counseling?" Julian liked solutions.

"We could," I said. "But not now." I also liked solutions, but solutions are like cheese—it takes time for the wetness to press out; it takes time for it all to cure.

We were naked, just getting out of bed. In fact, this nakedness was part of the problem—we were so casual about it all the time that I'd look at household things, like a jumble of boxes in the garage that never made it to the Goodwill, and I'd look at my husband's sex, and each seemed equally as ordinary and unimportant.

"I'm not asking for a divorce," I told him. "I just need some time." *Thunk.*

"You plan to come back," he said. It was helpful for me to hear Julian talk in this way; he spoke often to confirm or disconfirm. He had swung his legs over the side of the mattress and pulled his robe from the row of hooks above his nightstand.

I hesitated. "I think so. Yes."

I knew that my husband could stay very calm in crises. For example, in an earthquake, he would be the one who would remember which doorways were loadbearing and therefore the best to take shelter under. If trapped in debris, he would actually have a whistle with which to alert rescuers. He would produce this from his pocket along with water purification tablets, flares, high protein snacks, and compress bandages. He would also, despite perhaps being pinned in the wreckage, be able to reach his pocket to retrieve these items, and he would know not to actually light the flares, lest the spark of a match ignite the combustibles from ruptured gas lines.

"What about Anne?" he asked. Our daughter. Her name was Anastasia but we had followed the trend of giving girls old-fashioned names and then making the name cute, like Ellie for Eleanor, Abby for Abigail, and so on. He had not liked my idea that we could go with Dorky for Dorcas, even though I had a great aunt Dorcas.

"*Dorcas* means *gazelle*," I had told him.

"I like Gazelle better," he had said.

I put on a shirt and a pair of athletic pants. "I can't take Anne," I said. "I think she will be okay with just you for a while. She likes you."

"Of course she likes me," Julian said.

"Not all kids like their parents," I said. "But she likes you. You are lucky with that."

"She's only three. She doesn't know not to like me," he said.

"I doubt it," I said.

"This is strange, Laura," he said. "I feel like this is the first I've heard of it. I feel like this is sudden." He cinched his robe. It was plaid.

I wanted to say, *I have tried to speak to you and you have elected not to listen.*

I wanted to say, *By the time you get home in the evening, I have had so much vodka that I don't care.*

I wanted to say, *Enjoy the second shift!*

I would have meant any of these things, but in truth, Julian was kind to me and to Anne, in an old-fashioned way—he came home late and often excused himself to our shared office to work some more, but I believed more that he had poor time-management skills and a traditional man's allegiance to work than that he was actually avoiding us. And, I also wasn't sure how much any kind of explanation would be helpful. What could I say, really, to help explain why I did not want to wake up next to him?

"Do you want some coffee?" he asked, always civil.

I nodded.

Julian tightened his robe again as he passed me, heading for the kitchen. I had given him the robe when we were new. In fact I had stolen it from someone who I'd thought of as my last hurrah before settling into a serious life. I'd let the guy pick me up at a bar; he was dressed nicely with a pretty smear of gray around his temples. I still liked that look—someone who is just on the cusp of getting older. There is something about our turn from one place to another, like girl to young woman, man to gentleman, which brings our sex out.

As Julian rummaged around in the kitchen—grinding the beans, measuring water—I remembered how I'd casually lifted the Nordstrom bag that held what was now his robe on my way out of that stranger's house. There had been a gift receipt inside, and Julian had been ultimately too polite to exchange it even though the color was not exactly right for him.

After we had our coffee, awkwardly, and Julian went to work, I did leave. It was only for a week and a half, not enough to really amount to much. I went to Washington's Olympic Peninsula—the arm of the state that sticks out into the Pacific. On a map it looks like the edge of paper, torn the way children without scissors will, with a bead of saliva down the crease, ragged and wet. Also, it was October, so the water and the sand and the sky were all very gray.

I didn't do much but drink wine on the porch of a dumpy condo. I watched the blur of the surf into the coastline and clouds, and I considered how maybe sameness did not have to mean stasis.

Then I went home, and when I unpacked my bag, I put it back in the closet in the same place, and I hung all of my clothes on the exact same hangers I had taken them from.

I refused to believe it was something about marriage. It was something about us and the everyday: the longer Julian and I were coupled, the more I developed indifference to the body. We'd been passionate once, but increasingly I thought of this like the messes that were accumulating in more and more corners the longer we lived in our house—when we first moved in, the immediacy of any kind of clutter was unbearable to me; later, it became inconvenient; finally, there was a settling.

Our bodies, like any other piece of household effluvia.

Here is the stove.

Here is the laundry.

There was my breast.

It was almost like a miracle that we'd conceived Anne, not a sacred one, but one of statistics. I felt a kind of guilt about it, with so many people who struggled, who timed their copulations around ovulation and injected themselves with the urine of women already pregnant.

Early in the pregnancy, I took down a framed painting from one wall in our office and then leaned it against the opposite wall. I was only going to move it—it was too heavy in the original space and made the room feel like it was tilting. When Julian asked me what I was doing, he said that it was just me, that the room was certainly not tilting.

"I said it *feels* like it is tilting," I told him, "not that it is *actually* tilting."

"I don't see it," he said. "But I don't care if it gets moved."

"Maybe you're used to it," I said. "Like people who have one leg longer than the other and they never really know until they go to a chiropractor because their back hurts."

Julian gave me a blank look.

"They think it's their back because they're used to the leg," I said.

"If one of my legs were longer than the other, I would know," Julian said.

I gave him this. He was a scientist; he might have been right. He might have already measured.

"I'll let it sit for a few days," I said. "We can see how it *feels*."

Years later, though, the painting remained unhung. His mother had given it to us; it had been in her house for many years, and had been bequeathed to us with much ceremony. A landscape in a gold laminate frame, it was the kind of thing that gets thrown out when people pass, but for now it was with us.

Occasionally I would vacuum underneath and behind it, where it was making an ever-deeper groove against the plush. Sometimes I would even clean the glass, but I got used to the way it looked in the office, and finally, Julian stacked a box of files in front of it.

Our collections, our dust in the atria.

Even after Julian's mother died we did not throw it out, as by then it had become another layer in our unsteady foundation, a sediment of glass and old shoes and dirty sheets, held together by nothing but static.

There were times that I thought sex with Julian might be like exercise or healthy eating or reading the classics or driving a stick-shift—things that can be hard to get started on but become easier with practice, stimulating even. Or like growing a vegetable patch; once the long wait for spring is over and the seeds have been started, the transplanting complete, the frequency of watering gauged, the garden is sustaining. The memory of crisp lettuce propels a whole host of other activities, like changing the design of the plot or contemplating the reproductive life of aphids.

Before I met Julian, in my last semesters of college, I'd spent a year feeling a little predatory. It wasn't that I pursued anyone relentlessly or illegally or was especially horrible towards men, but I would meet them and I would sleep with them. I had so much energy for this and no energy for anything beyond it. It wasn't only the excitement of the casual, it was also the pitch of it. One clear note that did not sustain.

Then I met Julian. He was in the student union. All I did was say hello to him, in passing. He was wearing the same university sweatshirt that I was.

He said hello back to me. He said, "Didn't we take an astronomy class together?"

"Yes," I said, though I did not actually know if this was true.

"I thought you were familiar," he said.

"Yeah," I said. I was familiar. I was a familiar, ordinary person wearing brownish hair and a college sweatshirt.

And when I saw him again, a few days later, we again exchanged hellos, and he invited me for coffee.

"Is that too weird?" he asked.

"I never think coffee is weird," I said. "I love coffee." This was true.

So we went to a local place, and then later we took a drive and ended up fucking in the back of my car, which was a hatchback with the back seats perpetually down.

"I didn't really mean to go that far," Julian said to me when we were done.

"Me neither," I said, but I had. I was young then but I wasn't an idiot—I'd grown up on a farm, so I didn't believe these things just happened. I mean that I believed in the pure pull of biology, but that even an old milk cow will dance around a little for the aging bulls if she is open, whether she can really carry a calf or not.

By then I'd already had many of these kinds of lovers—these easy, one-date men. They were not difficult to find, especially because I was like them. Julian was different. He insisted that he take my phone number. He insisted that I accept his. He called me every day for a week.

As I saw more and more of him, he calmed me. He was level.

Indeed, his legs were perfectly plumb.

Our courtship felt habitual before habit had even had time to form.

We said our vows quietly, at the courthouse, with no one but the state-appointed witness in attendance.

I took these things to be a sign of love—the inward turn, the lack of declaration in the smell of the clerk's triplicate papers, the quiet legality.

I thought this was the other side of all those uncomplicated fucks—an uncomplicated husband made with a simple signature.

I held Julian's hand on our way to a late lunch. It was April, and misty. I was a damp bride in bad shoes. The dim light of the afternoon fell onto Julian from the side, and the light off him was just as dim, like a prism without enough angles to refract.

Later in my pregnancy when Anastasia had grown enough for her features to come through clear on a sonogram, I'd wondered if my husband was really her father. Then, he was working as a geologist at an environmental organization. I hadn't been unfaithful to him, but I did have trouble accepting that this man of precision and exacting recycling standards was really capable of fathering a girl with such a fine, watery face.

It wasn't until the contractions came on strong—after Julian's workday but before he had changed out of his suit—that I was sure she was half his. She was already a girl made of accidentally impeccable timing, a trait she would have gotten from her father, so it seemed appropriate that she would arrive without inconvenience.

She arrived early in the morning, just as the spring sky was lighting up. I was surprised at how quickly they took her from me. There had been part of me that had wanted to have her at home, away from the chill of a hospital and aggressive scalpeling, but I had also, growing up, seen many births—mostly of cattle and swine—and more than making me comfortable with the idea, I was terrified. Though it usually doesn't, much can go wrong. There can be a great deal of screaming. There can be blood. I felt close to the idea that birth is a place where two worlds are opened at the same time. I was happy that Anne had come to us in the morning rather than the twilight.

Julian decided that he would go to work directly, unshaven and in the same clothes as the day before.

"You could stay here," I said to him.

"You should rest," he said. "And your mother will be here before too long."

"But they'll understand, Jules, if you take a day off," I said.

"I'm fine," he said, "I can get through my day."

It would only be fair to say that the kiss he planted on my forehead was sweet, that he closed the door gently on his way out. Julian was kind and Julian was smart, but there were certain things he could not see.

I didn't want to sleep either, for the first time in too long. I wanted to be awake with him, with our new girl.

I understood that he needed the normalcy of his office but I didn't like it.

Life continued to be normal with Anne. We were assured sleepless nights were normal, and I breast fed normally: for a year, somewhere between the minimum requirements and the cut-off of getting too old for it in public. I worked at a university, so I took my maternity leave and then I went back and had the advantage of flex-time, and I was appropriately grateful for the school's reasonable expectations of a mother employed outside the home.

Anne hit her developmental marks.

Julian started a consulting firm with a friend.

By the time we celebrated her second birthday, I had completely lost any ability I had left to get angry.

So when I left him, even for such a short time, it wasn't out of rage. I hadn't been able to get mad at the way being a mother had changed my emotional life, and I hadn't had a chance to rail against the inequalities of female versus male parentage—really, I had it pretty easy. Really, there wasn't much for me to go on a tear about. But if there was, I couldn't feel it.

Mostly, it was hard for me to engage.

The household and my life with Julian had gone infestive, like zebra mussels or mint.

Grime in the ventricles, earth in the aorta.

I still had some friends and I was deeply envious of most of them. I saw how instead of sinking into the dustbunnies of their more adult life, they'd warmed to it and kept the corners swept clear.

No beggar's velvet, no slut's wool.

Mostly, when I was gone from my husband and daughter, I missed my daughter. And from my perch on the condo porch at the seaside I hoped that he would find her difficult.

I knew she would spend most of the time at daycare, which she liked. I knew that Julian would spend most of his time at his office, which he liked. I also knew even with a short absence he would take more to her, because he would have to.

I wanted this both because I thought Anne deserved a present father and because I didn't want Julian to think he could be spared the emotional life of girls. He didn't get to just disappear into his work. She was not a demanding child, but she was still a child, and there were things that needed to be done, like picking her up on time, and carefully combing her hair, and shielding her from the boring ugliness of adults.

When I came back, there was also the feeling that nothing had changed. I shouldn't say I *came back*. I should say I unpacked my suitcase. In the evenings, we still sat silently across from each other at the table, and we listened to our daughter chirp away about her day in the toddler language that only we three shared.

I had learned that I'd been wrong about my reasons for staying married to Julian. So far I didn't know how to do anything about it. For years I had thought that his patience and his composure had been good for me. He had tamed me and I thought this was trust.

Now I felt deeply dishonest.

I also thought I probably still knew the difference between the flash of heat that comes with infatuation and the enduring kind of devotion that can keep two lives together.

And Julian was very devoted. He could have easily filed papers at any time. He knew the kinds of people who were good at these things. I knew the kinds of people who drank too much in an attempt to self-medicate their ennui, and who called it such. Julian's friends had walls of dry-cleaning protecting them against all the things that might really be going on, mine had their jobs with students and in the sheltered world of non-profits.

I wasn't entirely sure that having Anastasia had made me a better person. It had made me a different person. Without her, I might have been able to leave Julian for longer. Without her, I might also not have noticed how slow and predictable our patterns had become, how our blood had turned to dirt. I didn't have a longing for my old life, but rather a deep reservation about where we were going.

I thought maybe I could finally put the picture back up in the hallway or do some intense organizing—change the weight of the house, the slope of it. When I'd gotten new tires on my car, I'd seen the technician wedge little lead weights between the rim and the rubber. Julian described to me the difference between static and dynamic balance and that most shops were converting to zinc instead of lead because of the environmental impact.

Very simple and clever, I needed some of these.

Scraps of something hard to lace into the wobbly bits.

This would smooth me, if there ever came a time of increasing speed.

Even After Fire, the Daylight Comes

Jenny was young when her father left—but for one picture in a scrapbook her mother kept (the stranger-man cradling a baby to him, his hand covering his head, his eyes looking straight to the camera, not to her) and the features in Jenny's face that she could find no anchor for on her mother's, she did not know him.

Jenny was already growing tall. Her mother was also tall. Her mother had played basketball at school, a few years after Title IX. Then, the only thing longer than her mother's hair was her legs. She said she hated wearing dresses but she wore them anyway because she could never find pants that came to the correct spot on her ankles.

Jenny knew the story of her father leaving, what there was of it. One night, her mother had turned in early, taking baby Jenny with her. They had a bassinet but Jenny was fussy, so her mother brought her to the bed, where they slept well enough. They both woke at the same time in the morning. Jenny opened her tender brown eyes to the new light in the bedroom and her mother said, *Good morning, honey girl.* When her mother looked at the spot on the other side of the sheets, she knew her husband hadn't slept there. She scooped her daughter into her arms and lifted her shirt. She left the room with her daughter content on her breast and she checked the house—a small, tidy house, a modest house—and she found no trace of her husband. She checked again, it didn't take so long to look twice, but still, no one, and she checked a third, this time stepping out into the yard, peeking into the backseat of the car and noting that his truck was absent, sweeping the shower curtain aside, just in case he had drank too much and, in the dead heat of summer, fallen asleep against the cool of the porcelain. She checked the closet: a duffle bag, gone. She noted a few swinging hangers which she was sure had held shirts the night before. She checked the tin where they kept grocery money and found it empty, Jenny still at her breakfast.

It was Saturday. She sat at the empty kitchen table. She looked at the phone on the wall but it did not sound. She looked at the beer cans in the bin, but there was no rustling among the aluminum, no message for her. She hadn't known Jenny's father long. They'd met at a party on the riverbank that she'd gone to with some of her friends from school; it was the summer of their graduation. The house belonged to her parents, both passed, in a car accident, when she was a junior. That had been hard. She'd never wished for a sibling more in her life. She was glad that her grandparents were gone too, because even as a young person she understood how it was worse to bury a child, but she wasn't sure how to approach the arrangements, she wasn't sure how to handle everything. There was some money, her parent's savings, that could carry her for a while. The house was paid for. Her father had a small life insurance policy. Her mother had a dent in the side of her head that was large enough to nix an open casket.

After the river party, Jenny's father had come around some. Jenny's mother worked at a construction company, in the office. She did paperwork for permits and the field crew schedule. When she had told him she was pregnant, he put her in his pickup and they went to the courthouse. She'd worn the same maroon dress she wore on her high school graduation day because it was her only good dress. Her aunt had bought it for her. It had come in the mail, from J.C. Penney. He wore his work boots and his cleanest pair of jeans and a shirt he'd borrowed off a friend.

She hadn't loved him when she signed her name on the paperwork, and she hadn't loved him when Jenny was born. Her job was nice about letting her take a few weeks off. She missed her mother. Her mother, canning cherries. Her mother, brushing her hair until the shine came up. Her mother, giggling when her father pinched her tush in the kitchen. Her mother, holding her hand on the porch on nights when the moon was not out, saying, *We named you Lucy Estelle, girl, because Lucy means* "born at daylight," *and Estelle means* "star."

Lucy Estelle kept Jenny close, the baby's skin warm on her skin. She had milk for her daughter and a solid roof. She had some money still, from the life insurance—only two years ago, but how time had passed—and she had the job at the construction company that was waiting for her.

Jenny knew that her mother had whispered to her then, *We'll be okay,* and rocked her until she had gone back to sleep, and they had both dreamt through the night, sure in each other.

Once, when Jenny was in the fourth grade, there was a blue pickup truck parked among the school buses and a man at the wheel. The man was watching out, it seemed, for every girl that passed, and Jenny felt the bottom part of her stomach drop. *Jenny,* she heard him call, *Jenny, I know you know me,* and she did know him, in the same way that he hadn't seen her in nine years but knew who to call out to. Her bus was just behind his truck, so she had to walk fully past him. *Jenny,* he called, *come say hello to your dad.* He reached across the cab and swung the passenger side door open. She was old enough to understand he was handsome, in his way. She was old enough to understand why she might hitch up her skirt and hop into his truck for a ride along the river, but she kept walking to her bus. *Jenny!* he called, and crawled across the bench seat and scrambled onto the school sidewalk. *Get in the truck,* he said, just as her foot touched the first step of the schoolbus stair, the door open wide for her.

"I'm your dad, get in the truck," he said.

"Can't," Jenny said. "Mom's waiting for me." The first word she had ever spoken to her father, *Can't.*

"I'll take you home directly," he said, squinting against the low, afternoon light.

The schoolbus driver had her eye on her, seatbelt unbuckled, her hand extended.

"Mom's waiting," Jenny said again, because it was true.

"I promise I'll just take you straight home," he said, but the bus driver was out of her seat, pulling Jenny up the steps and hustling her into one of the rear seats and sitting her down next to a high school boy. *Watch her*, she said, and went back out to the man on the sidewalk, the man who was back climbing into his blue pickup, peeling out of the dirt-paved school lot, screeching through the intersection in front of the school, and barreling onto the highway, just like her mother had always said, not in a hurry for much, but to get out of there.

In seventh grade, she went to Denver for a science fair. She placed third in her school's contest, for a project called "Fire & Burning." It was about the chemical reactions. She had lit matches, flicked lighters, even torched a pail of garbage (with her mother's permission) and then labeled and arranged her findings on a three-fold poster board. She hadn't worked that hard on the project, really—the other two winners had done much more than her. *Air Pressure / Water Pressure: Pressure Under Pressure* and *Gears: Compare the Effectiveness of Different Lubricants* won first and second, respectively. Jenny was a very distant third.

Still, she set up her poster board on her table in the auditorium. Her mother had sewn her a tablecloth cut down from an old sheet and sent through the wash with bright red powder dye and then trimmed in yellow rickrack. Jenny agreed the cloth gave her station flair, but she didn't believe it would actually help her rankings. Still, her mother was there, straightening the display, and beaming. And for just a moment, she thought she saw her father, slinking through the crowd, his heavy boots streaking the floor.

What did he know of sulfur, of phosphorus. She didn't need to win the competition, she only wanted to make a good showing—her mother was already proud. When the results were posted, Jenny's schoolmates ranked 10th and 11th, she far back at thirty-four of forty entries.

"I'm still happy for you," her mother said.

Born at daylight. Star.

Her mother was plasma held together with gravity. Her mother was thermonuclear fusion of hydrogen and supernova. Her mother knew fire.

"Thanks, Momma," Jenny said. She looked again for her father, as they packed the displays up. She would keep the tablecloth to drape over her dresser, and she would take it to college where she used it on an altar when she was experimenting with paganism, and she would have it with her years later when she married, the red long faded and the yellow border turned more to gray and the cloth so holey it had to be cut down and re-hemmed to handkerchief size. She wore the scrap in her garter, something old.

"Did you see him?" her mother said, when they drove home.

"No," Jenny said.

"He was here," her mother said.

"He wasn't," Jenny said. The car hummed.

Fire is the oxidation of material in the process of combustion.

Ash is the residue after a sample is burned and mostly salty.

Jenny knew that biology was strong, but it wasn't everything. If flame was the visible part of the fire, she closed her eyes to him. If heat was energy transferred from one place to another she was non-conductive, a shield to him. In the wild, fire burns clean through the understory, leaving the canopy of trees and clearing the ground for the newest, green shoots. The grasslands look leveled, at first. The forests look destroyed, at first. The dirt, scarred with charred seeds and blackened branches, seems barren until the smoke clears and the budding begins, pushing past the charcoal, into a clear expanse of sky. Whenever Jenny reached, it was with her mother's fingers laced through hers. Above them, damp, dew-heavy clouds. Above them, a rain.

When Jenny had her eighteenth birthday, her mother made a cake in their small oven, and put one candle on it, the wick hungry at the cheap, colored wax, drizzling onto the buttercream. The cake had risen high and light, and her mother had sung "Happy Birthday" in her low, trembling voice. They each had a corner piece, which was what they liked, and the rest of the cake remained like a partly toothless smile.

When she was Jenny's age, Lucy Estelle would have been grieving her parents and preparing for a baby. At her age, Jenny was unsure about what was next and happy to still have her mother's friendship, after everything. The house had hardly changed, there were some different curtains and cookware, but the structure was the same as the day when her grandparents had walked out the front door and locked the latch against their own not coming home. Lucy Estelle, without a key, because she'd never needed one since someone had always been home, waited for them on the steps until the sun went down, the air so dry her heart pumped dust.

Jenny had not gone far for college—the point was that she'd gone—just to the north, Fort Collins, on scholarship that barely covered costs, but barely was better than nothing. She lived in the dorms at first and while she didn't argue with the other girls, she didn't get on with them either. She kept to herself. She had already decided on a practical major, accounting. Her roommate, from Nebraska, was studying the classics, and she invited Jenny to nights of performance art with her troupe, but Jenny never went. She liked being alone in the dorm room or by herself at a table in the library. Her first year, she went home for the summer and camped in her old bedroom. She looked for a job, but found nothing, so she cooked for her mother, cleaned, and gardened. Her tomatoes grew high on their stake, her herbs bushy, her corn long and tall. She shucked the ears at the kitchen table, where she had done her homework for most of her life. She slept with a full belly in her childhood bed, wrapped in the same itchy sheets. Her mother was happy to have her home, proud again.

In the fall, she did not return to the dorms—too expensive, too tight. She rented a studio apartment close to campus in the renovated VA hospital. Her room had tile halfway up the walls and she thought it must have been a ladies room once, powder pink with gray grout. She liked sleeping in the apartment without the breath of her roommate. She liked having her own bathroom and a kettle that no one else touched. In the mornings she woke up and made herself coffee and sometimes smoked a joint over her tiny range, blowing the smoke through the rattly exhaust fan.

Once she heard a knock and she looked through the peephole and she swore she saw her father. She took a big gulp of air and undid the deadbolt, but when she opened the door there was nothing but air whooshing into an open hallway.

The second summer she did not go home because she wanted to keep the apartment. She had a part-time job at a deli and they told her they could have her on full through the summer since the other students were leaving. There was a man who washed dishes and had tattoos on his forearms who also worked there. He smelled like sweat and looked at Jenny in a way she couldn't name. He was close to her age, but he seemed older. He was a version of herself, if her mother had been more reckless, if her mother had not had the house and they had floated between sympathetic relatives and friends, with no place to call her own— or if her father had been around, bringing trouble and the rowdy neighbors. If that.

They went for coffee first, which turned to a night of beer back at her place. He didn't have a place, really. She couldn't work out if he was staying at the shelter near the deli or on the kitchen floor, but either way, he complimented her on her apartment, how clean it was, how cozy. The second time they started with beer and finished with whiskey, finished with Jenny saying she was so, so tired and crawling into her bed in the studio; in a studio the bed was always there, warning or invitation, and him, Richard, unlacing his shoes and peeling off his socks and crawling in next to her.

It was the first time she'd had a man in her bed, but she didn't tell him and didn't cry.

In the morning, he was up before her, cooking coffee on the small stove—like she did, the way she had learned from her mother—and digging through her cabinets.

"You want some biscuits, baby?" he said. "Got to say, I'm pretty impressed you have real butter."

"Sure," she said.

He brought her coffee and she propped up in a pile of pillows to drink it.

He made breakfast and she still was not out of bed, her thighs sticky and her breasts hurting. He sat with her while they ate, forks clinking against her secondhand stoneware.

He asked if he could use her shower before he left for his shift, and she loaned him a clean t-shirt. On his way out the door, he kissed her between the eyes on the forehead, and after he had latched the door she got up and saw that he had tidied up the kitchen. The bathroom was still steamy and warm and she washed slowly under the hot water, and when she got out she saw that he had left his dirty shirt folded on the back of the toilet tank. It smelled like the deli and the detergent they used and him.

For the rest of the summer, Richard was in her apartment. She saw the lines around his eyes get a little softer, especially when he mentioned how nice it was to have a regular place to stay. Jenny got softer too, in the belly, from his cooking. At the deli, they were nice to each other in the same way all of the employees were nice—they depended on one another to keep the place going, and everyone needed the job. In early July, she gave him a key to her apartment and she came home from her late shift to find him making sandwiches in the kitchen that he wrapped in wax paper and tucked into his knapsack.

"Let's go to the park and watch the fireworks," he said. "America's birthday."

"I'm tired, Rich," she said.

"Everyone's tired. Gunpowder will help."

They walked to the river park and spread out on a blanket, and Richard held her hand. He had tattoos on his fingers and up his forearms, one on his back, one on his stomach, deep blue ink just like the summer light that never seemed to get all the way to black.

She thought when school started again in fall she wouldn't see him anymore. She wouldn't have time for lazy mornings or late nights. He hadn't started to talk about a future—the closest he got was to stop asking her if it was okay if he stayed the night—that had happened when she offered the key. She liked seeing him sleeping in her bed. She liked that when the cashiers at the deli split up their tips to the backroom staff he dropped his share of quarters into her laundry jar. She washed his apron and his jeans with hers and folded his shirts into perfect, neat squares. He had the knapsack and a duffle bag that was parked under her bed. Everything he owned fit inside. She told him about growing up, the house, her mother. He didn't tell her his story—when she asked about his parents he always said, *another time*, so she stopped asking. She told him he should study to be a cook if he was going to work in kitchens, there were better jobs out there, not just a cook, she said, a chef.

"Chef, shit," he said. "I didn't even finish high school."

"No?" she said, "How come?"

"It just happened that way," he said.

Jenny stopped by the university library the next day; it was so quiet during summer session.

"I'm not sure where to start," she said at the reference desk, "but my friend needs his GED."

"Oh, there's a whole section." The woman at the desk was a graduate assistant and took Jenny through the stacks, helped her find the curriculum guidelines and then sat with her while she used the computers to find a test site.

She went back to her apartment with a bag of books and a few printed pages from the internet, and waited for him.

"You could finish by the end of summer," she told him. "I made you an appointment for the exam."

"I don't know," he said, but he agreed to at least try.

There was enough room in the apartment for a small table, where Jenny did her homework. She started reading ahead for the fall term while Richard worked through grammar and math and social studies. She liked this life with him, quiet and marked by the sounds of pages turning, the scratch of a pencil against paper, the swoosh of an underline.

On the day of the exam, they had both requested to be scheduled off from work, and their boss raised an eyebrow.

"I don't like hanky-panky with the employees," he said.

"Got it," Jenny said. She rode the bus with him to the testing center at the public library and held his hand. He had his knapsack on his back and a notebook under his arm, just like any other student. It was August. He passed easily. They celebrated with cheap champagne and stir-fry.

She was grateful to him when September came. He didn't make her ask for her key back or make her pick a fight. She came home from the late shift and his duffle bag was gone from where it had peeked out from under her bare bed frame and the key to the apartment gleamed on the table, resting in the center of a piece of torn notebook paper. *Thank you, Jenny*, he had written, and signed his name with a heart around it.

He hadn't said anything in the few hours their shifts crossed that day, and he hadn't said anything to her the night before, only held her, so close there was nothing but heat between them. She took some quarters from her laundry jar and went to the corner to call her mother. The phone rang until the answering machine picked up and Jenny could picture the house perfectly, her mother's voice sounding through the empty rooms.

The Seven Stages of Anger

1. NEON

When you kissed me under the lights of the cinema, I wondered how it had been that I had never known you, that I had never tasted your taste of lavender and star anise and coffee black, felt the pink of your hand on my face. I wondered how you had made me wait through Lorelei Lee's dancing on screen before you reached for me. I wondered how I had even found you, as I'd been snaking along, invisible, lighter than air, waiting for the electricity that would make me glow orange.

I felt it at first touch—the gas light.

Neon is produced by radioactive decay, is sometimes transmitted to Earth via the solar wind, and is found in terrestrial rocks and volcanic emissions. A noble gas, it isn't much without a current or a compound to bind with. It has no magnetic properties. With more than 40 percent of the refrigerating capacities of helium, neon can make you very, very cold. And diamonds. It is found there too.

2. LAMB'S WOOL

The sheep, it seems, is rarer. The lamb is coveted. The child. The lamb's meat, the *Agnus Dei*, the vales rejoicing, lying down with the lion, etc. The lamb's wool. Your hair was coarse and crimped like that. I remember sitting on my neighbor's dry porch, when I, too, was a child, carding and carding and carding, trying to help. I remember the first taste I had, a zillion miles from America, the Imam's voice cutting across the field of traffic as I held my skewered meat in my hands and the street vendor looked at me, smiling kindly, like he was practicing *zekât* (the giving of alms), like we were bending to pray.

If I could have, I would have woven a cloak from your hair; I would have cut it, cleaned it, washed it, dyed it. I would have combed it and spun it to thread and knotted each strand carefully on my loom. I would have wrapped myself in it whole, as a cilice, or as a shroud.

3. Peacock

It was fear that made me push when you tried to close me out. We were shoving, one on each side of the door. And caught in the underneath space—where light peeks into a darkened room—your toenail lifted from your skin as easily as plucking an eyebrow. We tried to stop the bleeding, and later I lay on the floor and cried, while what was left of your nail turned from red to blue to purple, like a god's eye.

There was blood on the floor, in the sink, on your shirtsleeve. Our faces, too, were down to the pink. We didn't know what we were fighting about after too many hours together and much too much liquor, but at some point you had spread out your tail, a matrix of glitter, and your irises, flashing from green to blue.

So, when you pushed on the door, it was natural that I'd push back. It was natural I'd want to get in on you; drawn to the shine and scared I might not see it again, ever, after what you'd said.

Male peafowl lift their feathers from the ground to court hens, and for the most part, their trains hinder their movements and drag through the dirt. But when I was young and my grandmother kept peacocks who shit all around the perimeter of the duck pond, we would throw rocks at them until we got their ire up, and they did nothing but shimmer back at us.

It is true. I am sorry for your digit, but not for the door and not for the stones.

4. TOPAZ

When her aunt died she gave me the gold band set with yellow topaz and the matching earrings she'd inherited. I never wore the earrings, in part because I lost one almost immediately. She kept the ruby set for herself, the first real jewels either of us had, handed down from a dead woman, and we wore these promises on our pinkies. I still slip mine onto the left hand, with my mother's defunct wedding band on my right—perfect costume jewelry—and I wonder about these women and their slim *digitus quartus*, me dancing or eating cheeseburgers in the secondhand baubles of country ladies.

And once you gave me a topaz, on a very slender chain, a gold chain as light as bean threads. Yours was different. Sparkling blue like an eye or prints of a building, roll after roll of perfect facsimiles.

When it is pure, topaz is another clear mineral; common imperfections tint it wine or straw. Blue takes something stronger: radiation.

I have her ring still, and I wore your necklace for as long as I could keep it. I wore it just above my heart, your laboratory rock, on different continents and in hotels as I followed Jupiter across the globe, or that is, as I looked for something that looked like someone who was in charge. Of the world. Or at least the weather.

I cannot say when, exactly, I reached last to finger the stone and discovered, like you and like my view of the great red spot, it was gone.

5. CARBON

From coal to diamond, I felt your load leaning into me.

Like bearing the weight of uranium almost, 92 protons and 146 neutrons, the heaviest naturally occurring element, you were the weight of everything, fizzing in cold water, turning my insides to mush.

My personal Windscale fire, melting anything from graphite to concrete.

I couldn't tell which you were, luster or black, hexagon or blaze.

What I did know was the home we shared turned sour. I was angry with you because *you were always there.* I would come around the corner and see your car in the drive, and I would think, *Oh, Christ.*

I was angry because you would have been in my bedroom in the day.

You had your own room, but there was mold growing on the mattress and piles of stinking laundry that you wouldn't clean up.

You *were always there* because you'd had a child, and when you moved to the city, chasing her father, we agreed to rent together.

So, you and her, sitting on my bed. My spare glasses bent. My smashed lipsticks. My spilled jewelry. Your crumbs. I loved your girl, actually, but she'd pull everything off the low shelves when she was angry at you, and you'd scream at her to stop. Every day.

You had run off from home at twelve because no one could own you. That was twenty years ago. You had gone back to that house a few times. You said you had three fathers, only one of them biological, living half a continent away, complaining about the price of cable.

You didn't understand why I was angry about the bedroom, why it mattered to me that you walked off with my pens, that there were sticky handprints around, that you read my notes.

Maybe you'd never had privacy.

So, no one could own you, and no one could own anything. You *were always there* because it was your home too. Your dark hair plugged the drains. Your half-eaten apples on the counter. The second child I heard you make.

You went the miles back to California from Washington.

I didn't talk to you again.

But I knew you were there in the heat and the pressure, carbon changing.

Your daughter, your allotrope.

You would holler at her, but you held her close—tight enough to squeeze her to crystal, to kerosene.

Watch her. She will be like you, and she will either turn hard or she will flame.

6. Tongue

So, you opened your mouth to me, jaw clicking wide, like a drawbridge coming down.

I tasted more than the salt of your tongue, more than the sweat of my own body, from where you'd kissed me there between the legs.

You put your tongue on my tongue. You put your mouth on my ear, and I listened to you whisper, the way your breath on my skin calmed me.

Our tongues are made of skeletal muscle and descend deep into the throat. Like the arm of an octopus, the tongue contains no bony support. There are four kinds of papillae on the tongue, and these house the buds: *filiform* (thread shaped), *fungiform* (mushroom shaped), *circumvallate* (ringed circle), and *foliate* (ridges and grooves).

The part of your tongue I think you liked best was *bitter*.

As in eating watercress and drinking tonic water. I wanted to tell you that Europeans had been using quinine as a prophylactic as early as the 1600s. By 1631 quinine was being shipped from Peru to Rome to treat malaria.

You took yours with gin.

But of course I believed you when you'd pull my head down to your lips and tell me you wanted me to conceive.

Then later, when the results came, I had acid in my mouth, *sour*.

My breasts hadn't fit inside my jacket for weeks. Your skin had that sleepy texture, shiny like pulled taffy, damp as sand.

We talked this over, hands at my abdomen.

You held my head in your palm. You kissed me like you could swallow me. You kissed me like one dog licking another dog's wounds.

Days later we had that baby cut right out of me.
And then we went home: my empty belly, your forked tongue.

7. Chameleon

Like you and the other fairskinned among us, I've spent days
hiding from sun. Because it is strong enough to sanitize surgical
tools or core an eye like an apple, we keep the ultraviolet off our
skin. We are the type who swig our vitamin D, pick it gingerly
off from fish's bones, search for chanterelles in the newly burned
woods.

Our ancestors had their sun gods, we have our SPFs.

The chameleon can see ultraviolet light and, in it, relaxes and
breeds. The pinhole eye rotates at 360 degrees, and they look
through to another spectrum.

The Earth lions are like us. Sexually, females differ from
males, both in outward behavior and in appearance. Their skin
pales or deepens in color in fear, in shame, in lust. Some birth
their young live. They do not hear.

For our part, you mashed the helmet on over your red hair,
you told me to turn and stare at the wall while you fired up the
arc welder; even faced the wrong way, the glimmer of metal
joining metal was obvious, the back of my head lit in white. I
would hum along with the electricity, while you looked through
your glass shield.

When I faced you again, you'd be surrounded in scraps,
welding beads, and spent electrode sticks, slag.

Like other reptiles, birds, and arthropods, chameleons
periodically molt.

Under feet, these husks of skin, of feather and exoskeleton,
crush more easily than even eggshells, crumble like poorly dried
clay. And though we may marvel at the remaining shape of the
body when the body has moved on, the finch, the lobster, and
the chameleon know enough to leave it behind.

Maps of the Americas

When she was in fifth grade, they did their lessons in portable classrooms with squeaky walls and floorboards full of soft spots. She disliked, intensely, the school. In the spring and summer, her desk was always dusty because the classroom windows were open, and the wind blew off of the Front Range in pressurized, howling bursts, carrying specks of grit, which Melanie was sure was made up mostly of dead moths and rotten leaves. Out the windows they had a view of the Rockies, but she could live without it. She'd rather have the glass tucked into the casements and the blinds down, out of the glare and the gusts. At school they told her she was lucky to live in a place like Colorado, where the sun shone often and the mountains kept watch over them, but all she had to do was look in any direction but west to see nothing but grass and flatland sprawl and the Platte snaking pathetically along, like when the boys peed onto a dirt clod at recess and then jumped back so they wouldn't get their own piss on their shoes. At school they said that if you asked a kid in a big city where meat came from that he would say, *The store*, and so children in the west should feel proud they possessed more survival skills, more expertise in the natural. Melanie did not feel proud, and as far as she was concerned, meat did come from the store. They took a field trip to a ranch once, but it wasn't like her parents kept a beef in the backyard. Usually they got everything at Costco.

Melanie thought it was boring, school, but she couldn't see what else she could do. She wanted to get on with it, but she understood she was a child and that part of being a child was years of waiting. At lunch, she ate in the cafeteria alone or with a friend and was depressed by the plastic trays and the plastic sandwich bags and the plastic smell of the food that had been either in the coat closet all day or recently scooped from a vat. It was hard not to feel like it was wasting her time. Every other Friday, hot lunch was pizza and maple bars, and these days were the worst because the entire school reeked of industrial pepperoni and fake syrup.

The school was in a suburban spot outside of Denver with a tiny historic main street surrounded by low-slung suburbs, and her parents lived in a one-story ranch with pretty shutters and clean eaves. They'd bought the house when they were newlyweds and could now afford more, but they loved the rooms and didn't want to move. Some of her best memories were of the improvements they made, months of new dust softening the edges—like her mother's powder, like glitter shaken from a jar. One year they put in another window in the kitchen to catch the early light, and her mother grew philodendrons in a line of clay pots on each windowsill. Her mother staked the vines until they were beyond the height of the walls, and then her father screwed hooks into the ceiling at tidy, six-inch intervals, each curve of tin cradling a rope of green. Melanie's mother watered faithfully and new leaves unfurled, the vines constantly reaching. It seemed important when it was time to mount a new hook. Her father would use his measuring tape for accurate distance, and little bits of the popcorn finish would scatter onto the kitchen tiles. Melanie remembered being lifted so she could pull the vine into its new support; it was like they had accomplished something. Another six inches, some proof that life was moving forward, even if it was only to the other side of the room.

Sometimes, she was surprised when she visited her friends' homes and the kitchens were dark and wallpapered or decorated with roosters—she loved the lush of their vines, and in the library at school, she learned that her mother's houseplants were poisonous to cats, and Melanie kept this as one of the many secrets an only child has. When she walked through the kitchen, rummaging for dry cereal or a glass of juice, she thought of the chemical danger and imagined herself feline, padding safely out of reach on the jungle's linoleum floor while her mother cooked whole chickens in a Dutch oven, stewed eggplants.

There were three bedrooms, and a half bath off the master. The carpets had been replaced and the old paper steamed off. Her parents helped her paint her room whenever she felt like it, and she went through coats of green, purple, cream, and finally yellow, taping the trim carefully and putting down a drop cloth to catch any errant blobs on the floor. She liked living there, the big backyard and her mother's irises—there were fresh flowers all summer in a vase on the kitchen table, and in the winter cuts from the philodendrons rooting in murky water.

Her father traveled for work sometimes, enough that they missed him but not so much that they didn't know him. He sold medical devices, and this, to Melanie, seemed like a very important job, because what if your heart stopped and no one had the paddles to get it going again? Her father solved this problem. On nights he was gone, her mother would put on her records, and they would sing along to Stevie Nicks or Carole King, waiting for their pork chops to finish.

In the living room they had a comfortable sofa and a few chairs. Sometimes the three of them would sit on the sofa and watch television, Melanie nestled in the middle. Sometimes they would work on the house, small chores like replacing the peephole or reworking the hinges of a sticky door. She liked these jobs, sitting on a low work stool in the garage with her father, polishing a cabinet pull or greasing an old drawer slider with paraffin until the glide was perfect. She had her own screwdriver with a pink handle and a small hammer that her father taught her to hold correctly, with her hand in the wide part of the grip, low to the base, to get the most leverage.

After school, her friends did cheerleading or basketball, but she would sit in the library, or on nice days take her books to the park and read. When Melanie's father was traveling, she liked to meet her mother where she worked as a teller, her fingers greased in glycerin from the tubs of pink Sortkwik, slips of deposit waiting for tally. She would walk through the empty drive-up window and press the call button so someone would unlock the doors.

The bank was order. Drawers of currency, counted. Bags of coin, rolled. Her mother was head teller, so she was always there late with the cash drawers. It was quiet after-hours, and there was something calming about her mother's expert handling of money—the way she could, after years of practice, spot old dimes made of real silver or wheat cents, measure fifty-bill bundles by weight or by running her thumb along the edge of a stack. Her mother asked her if she knew why all of the presidents faced right on coin except for Abraham Lincoln's mug on the penny. Melanie did not know. Alone, her mother would confirm her own work in an electric counter with two clawed wheels that whooshed like a half-open window in a speeding car. When Melanie was at the branch, she would load the hopper, verifying pile after pile, waiting for her mother to err, which so far had never happened. She came to love the incongruousness of it: someone who made just over clerk wages working through thousands of dollars with more expertise than the richest gangster. Her mother didn't actually care that much for money, but had the lingo anyway: A hundred bills was a *strap*, a thousand a *brick*. Melanie learned the treasury colors; she liked the wrappers for the twenties and hundreds the best, violet and mustard. At school, they had taken a field trip to the Denver Mint, and she felt superior because she already knew about money in large quantities, moving quickly.

At the end of the day, if her mother was in a good mood, they would walk home, arms linked, chatting. She would tell her about what she hated about school: her teachers, who were as interesting as a bar of soap, and how she had gotten in trouble for saying out loud that she thought studying American colonialism was boring.

"They boiled shoe leather in the winter at Jamestown," Melanie said. "I'd rather eat a dog."

"They had probably already eaten the dogs," her mother said.

"The map I drew of the settlement was mostly brown," Melanie said. "I left some blank spots because there was also a lot of snow."

Her mother told her stories of trying to educate her elderly customers on how to use debit cards and explained why she alone couldn't open the safe (because half of the employees knew the beginning of the combination, and the other half knew the end).

When her mother was in a bad mood, they made their way down the sidewalk side by side, both staring at the pavements Melanie knew by heart—here was the square that looked like something heavy had been dropped on it; here was the one with the concrete cracked in the shape of a star.

It's not too far, she thought, *the space between happy and sad.*

At night her mother would peel off her stockings and rummage in the kitchen. The thing Melanie didn't like about her father traveling was that it made her mother agitated. Sometimes they did work on the house projects, but the rooms seemed empty. She wondered what it had been like before her and what had been in her room, but she didn't ask.

Emptiness was the idea she liked most—the floors glossed and the walls a shell pink, the air kept fresh by a slow-moving ceiling fan. Probably they had used it for storage or something worse.

Once when her father was gone, they spent a week in school on Ponce de León arriving in Hispaniola and continuing on to Florida, searching. Pierced by an arrow anointed in poisonous sap from a manchineel tree, he took his last breath in Havana. *Who cares*, Melanie thought, but she colored in her hand-drawn map of the Caribbean anyway—in school they always drew maps, and Melanie's mother saved them all in a poster tube in the hall closet—making a hashed line to mark de León's travels.

"It looks like a heart," her mother said, putting beef roast with a crown of perfect onions on the table. Her father had not called, Melanie knew, because her mother slammed the pan.

"It's not," said Melanie. "It's just a circle and then he dies."

"He was the one who was looking for the Fountain of Youth, right?"

"He didn't find it," Melanie said, rolling up the paper.

"Thank God," her mother said. "Who'd want to do this crap forever?"

But on the next night, he did come home. The weather was nice and so they had leftover roast sandwiches with horseradish on the patio. The earlies were in bloom, and the daffodils rimmed the yard like a corona.

Melanie liked the way the food looked, spread on the glass table, and she liked it when her father was there with them. When he traveled, it was not only his body gone; there was less sureness in the house.

When she was in sixth grade, her parents sat her down on the center spot on the sofa and turned two chairs to face her: They would separate, they had decided, and the house would have to be sold. Her mother's face was caved in, like bread punched down after it has risen. Her father looked like nothing, almost, a tiny fleck of flaked-off veneer. The house felt loose to her then, the years spent oiling creaks and tightening joists unraveling in a moment, the tiers of birthday cake and fluffy soufflés collapsing to wobbly floorboards.

What is this place, Melanie wondered then, *without us?*

It was the first days, after, that were the hardest. The wind would blow and Melanie would feel it in every real and imagined crack in the house; she would feel it in her body. Her mother came home with banker boxes and rolls of tape; her father hit the road, off to Omaha, Topeka, St. Louis. A Realtor came and drove a sign into the front lawn. It was fall and Melanie came home from school one day to the white post and the red letters of *For Sale* and the leaves swirling around the place where the stake had pierced the grass.

She packed her things very carefully, wrapping even the softest items in a cushion of newspaper and a protective layer of cellophane tape. She filled the boxes slowly, labeling with a permanent marker, and her mother did not rush her. It didn't seem like there was much in her room, but it was surprising how much a small space could hold. When she was finally finished, her mother asked her to help with the rest of the house. Some things Melanie was instructed to pack, some she bagged for the Salvation Army. They also had a pile near the entryway that belonged to her father: mostly a heap of clothes and tools with a half-used tin of mineral oil on the top, leaking onto his old trousers.

While Melanie was sorting knickknacks and wiping windowsills, it was hard for her not to catalog improvements that needed to be made: a loose screen, an almost imperceptible ding in the drywall. She wanted spackle and her screwdriver. She wanted her father to return from traveling with a sheaf of orders, her mother to core apples for a pie, and the three of them to set out to repairing a bit of scratched hardwood, all on their hands and knees with putty knives and sandpaper, her parents stooped to a height close to her own.

In the kitchen her mother was on a stool, loosing the philodendrons from their hooks, the vines in a coil in one hand like a lasso. It was terrifying to see the plants come down, the ceiling pitted and water-stained. She stepped down to push the stool closer to the wall and then climbed it again to start on another section. Melanie heard her mother talking, under her breath, *goddamn you, goddamn you.* It was rare for her to be angry like this, but even then Melanie knew. She was old enough to have already have been stung by the nasty boys who talked her into showing her panties one day, her best friend the next, all while the meaner girls looked on, laughing.

The tangle of ties and hex wrenches by the door was growing, and still they had not touched the garage. Melanie had trouble with the pile—half of which was just household junk her mother had decided belonged to her father now. The pile was not like him. It was disorganized. She kept working. It was the first time she had moved and the first time her mother had moved in many years, so they were slow.

She had a girl in her class who would take anything apart. Melanie herself had donated a cassette player she thought was ruined and an alarm clock that she had dropped so part of its guts were exposed through the chipped plastic shell. This girl returned the cassette player—reassembled and working—but pronounced the clock a goner. She didn't really care so much about fixing things; she said she liked to understand how they worked.

Melanie thought if she got this girl to help her take the house down board by board, they would not find the same answer, like a malaligned gear or cracked soldering.

In the living room, there was an end table that had not been packed and on the bottom shelf, a bowl of restaurant matches. Melanie selected one of her favorites, a blue cover and the inside match heads as silvery as snow. She squeezed the rest of the leaking mineral oil onto her father's things and struck one of the phosphorus tips until it flamed. Her hands were shaking, but she managed to ignite the entire book and launch it onto her father's things, which caught quickly with their sheen of petroleum. There was a *whoosh* as the oxygen sucked away from her.

She inhaled heat and wondered if her father's breath caught too, ash on her face, ash in his lungs.

When the smoke detector sounded, her mother came running, a torn philodendron vine laced through her fingers. There was a fire extinguisher still in the hall closet, and it took just a second to dampen the flames. They stood there for a minute while the foam settled around them. Melanie could see that the wall was stained black.

The girl at school was not really her friend, but sometimes they ate lunch together. When Melanie had gone to her birthday party this year, she was the only kid who showed up. The girl told her that day that her parents sometimes got angry at her, for example, when she had smashed the casing to the microwave to get inside. They thought she was violent and odd. They thought she should just use the buttons to heat up food, like everybody else.

"Are you okay?" her mother asked. She held the cylindrical red can like a weapon, out in front of her, fingers gripped tightly. The smell of burnt synthetics was deadly, and her mother's face looked more tired than anything.

"Do you have any more boxes?" Melanie asked. "We have a lot left."

"Sure," her mother said. She tossed the extinguisher onto the smoldering heap and led Melanie to the garage. "We'll be fine. You do the living room and I'll finish the kitchen. There are a few things in the bathrooms, and then the movers will come and we'll be gone."

"I'm sorry about the wall," Melanie said. "I could paint over it."

"It's your father's problem now," her mother said.

When the moving truck came, they took their boxes and some of the furniture and all of the plants and left the rest in a mess.

She wanted to feel anger when she got into her mother's car, driving away from the house for the last time, but she did not. She felt sad and in-between. They all loved the way the place had held them. Melanie was sorry for the scar up the wall, sorry for all the projects they'd never finish. She was sorry for the way the light fell as they followed the bumper of the moving van, the house shadowed under a canopy of cloud.

In their apartment, her mother still cooked, even if it was cheap stuff like frozen chicken breasts and canned sauce that she boiled down with leftover wine and garlic because buying six pounds of tomatoes was too expensive. Melanie would sit at the kitchen table and fiddle with her schoolwork while her mother sautéed. There was a gray light over the kitchen table and a gray light over the stovetop. The walls were gray from all the fat that had smoked off of all the meals that had been prepared by them and by other tenants, and Melanie's eyes were gray from the drudgery of school.

Sometimes she went to her father's. Usually this was during school breaks. He started traveling more, and he said his job made it too difficult to watch over her, though she did not think she needed much watching over. He also said that he had to work more to pay child support, but Melanie knew this wasn't true because she'd found his un-cashed checks tucked into an envelope in the kitchen junk drawer when she needed some batteries.

His house was much nicer than the apartment, but the time passed very slowly. He had a small outdoor pool, and in summers she liked to sit by it, the aqua reflected back at her and the water very still but stinking of chlorine. She liked to watch the shine when a small breeze came up, the tiny ripples when a wasp landed and broke the surface.

Sometimes her father wanted to get out of the house. That's how he would put it—*let's get out of the house*, he would say. He bought her a horseback riding lesson on a mangy, overworked pony. He took her to the park by the river, where they dutifully licked ice cream until there was nothing left of hers but a mushy cone. Once he sent her up in a carnival hot air balloon while he stayed on the ground. She knew she was supposed to pretend that she didn't know why her mother had left her father, but she saw the gloss on his eye when he looked at the girl taking tickets for the ride, who had on a dirty shirt and wasn't that much older than her. The carnival girl's father operated the balloon, and Melanie didn't want to go up in the air with him, but she did anyway, peeking over the basket as the man worked the burner and her own father became a small black spot. It was a sunny day, and the heat and the propane made her woozy.

Her father lived in his house alone, mostly. Occasionally there was a woman just leaving when her mother dropped her off, or someone pulling up the back drive when she was being picked up. Once Melanie had found a fresh lipstick in the hall bathroom. She put the lipstick in the refrigerator, right by his half-and-half, so he would know she had seen it.

In the balloon she wondered what would have happened if she had asked the carnival girl to come with her, if they had left their leering fathers on the ground to distract themselves, swapping stories, while their daughters sailed up until the rope was taut. What if the carnival girl had a penknife in her pocket and she sawed carefully through the tether, slicing the twists of jute one by one, until the balloon loosed and the two girls floated away, just another bright spot in the blinding sky.

Sometimes on the way home from school to meet her mother at the bank, Melanie would walk by the house. It wasn't exactly on the way, but if she was quick in the library and skipped her trip to the park, she could get to her mother in enough time that she didn't notice anything.

From the outside the house looked almost the same to her. There was new siding, but the same old eaves buckled under the weight of fall leaves, and there were brown spots on the grass from dog piss. The compression arm on the screen door had lost its snap, so it was always half ajar, like a warning.

She never saw anyone come in or out of the house, but the drapes had been changed and her mother's climbing rose knocked from the trellis. The house as she had known it had not been perfect, but she thought it could have been, if there had been more time.

The apartment was the first place they had come after the split, and Melanie figured they would be there for a long time. Her mother didn't ramble. In school they were studying the history of the Oregon Trail, and Melanie couldn't say that she preferred the politics of Westward Expansion over her mother's. They had been instructed to choose one stretch of trail and draw a detailed map of it. Melanie picked the last miles leading to Oregon City, the end of the line. Her map had a little key to mark points of interest—clean water, wild onion patch, blackberry grove. Her teacher thought this was very clever, so Melanie didn't tell her what she had really been thinking: *dead horse, poison oak, dysentery.*

Her father was more like the pioneers than her mother. He was the one who looked out across the horizon and wanted more than a small place to live and a tidy routine. The thing about the divorce was that her parents didn't seem any happier apart than they had together, just older.

In the balloon another thing she had thought about was jumping over the side. She didn't really want to do this, but she liked the idea of a freefall and the wind holding her, the look of shock on her father's face when she landed a few feet from him, hair windblown and eyes shut. The operator probably wouldn't have stopped her, though his daughter might have.

Once, not very long before the divorce, her father was supposed to come home on a Tuesday but he didn't. Her mother was making *coq au vin,* and it smelled like a miracle, chicken and wine and bay leaf. Maybe that was when she felt the first groan in the house, while the rooster stewed from tough to tender to tough again, and her mother waited for lights in the drive.

On that night Melanie selected the record—she loved Kim Carnes—and she sat in the dark with her mother while dinner burned.

Her mother had a story, about how she had met her father when he was fresh off his military service and been lucky enough not to see combat in Vietnam even though he was drafted in late 1969. In this story her mother was a brunette girl with legs up to *there*, and her father was handsome in his tattered green coat. They married quickly. Her mother had saved some money from her job working the food line in the hospital kitchen, and they put a down payment on the car her mother still drove, and they found the house. Once in a while on a long night, like the Tuesday her father didn't come home, her mother would have more cocktails than was customary, and she would tell Melanie that it was better to wait. It was better to see some of the world on your own first because marriage was hard.

Her mother hadn't waited when she was nineteen with blue eyes wide, so she waited with the stereo shouting love ballads and the oven sizzling. Melanie wanted her father to come home too, maybe even more than her mother did. She didn't know what was so hard about getting back to the house before dark; she did it all the time, and she didn't know what was out there that could keep him.

What is better than the candlelight on the mantel, she wondered, *the leaves on our vines?* She would have drawn a thousand more maps with reliefs shellacked in glitter, roads demarcated with more precision than the best cartographer, if any would have led him to them.

Ten Penny

M. used to come to me late at night, when he was stinking from the bar, all the alcohol and cigarettes and the heavy smell of desperation on his skin—he was like me and hated going home alone.

He would ring my bell, and I would let him in—his smile and those teeth as white and hard as picket; I'd never not let him in. I'd fix bourbon and roll a joint and climb up to the window seat with him, and we'd blow our smoke out at the city, my back against his chest. The window seat in my small apartment saved me. The window seat kept M. coming back, along with the promise of whiskey on fresh ice and mild narcotics and sticky sex on my low bed, though I think it was the view that held him. Looking onto the city buildings at night, he said to me what he was trying for: the same thing as a high-rise—keeping his lights on and reaching toward the sky. I'd push my face into his shoulder and hold my head there until I found it, under all that sweat and smoke, the smell of wood.

M. was a finish carpenter, though he could also frame. I admired his hands, which were long and slim and splintery and could feel out all the imperfections. There, at my elbow, the rough patch of scar from a decade-ago cycling accident—I remember sun and the dirt road and the deep drop down at my left, and then suddenly I was flying, and then suddenly I was stopped. M. knew nothing about how I lay on the road and bled, how I cried and cried at the falling, how I threw the bicycle into the ditch and walked into the little town nearby, how I never rode again, but he ran his finger around the ruined part of skin like he was a healer. He found the place on the back of my thigh, a puncture wound I got one day when metal collapsed around me; he touched the tiny dent above my eye, a fall onto a concrete step. He held my hand where it is crooked, outlined the asymmetrical ear.

These were the every time things. He couldn't stop himself from lingering around the broken places. M. was a man who built from scratch, who fit wood into wood without a seam.

One night he came, and it was no different, as we got stoned and he recapped his life since the last time I saw him. I gave him my own summary, and we sat in quiet for a few minutes, watching the traffic and the streetlamps. I knew more about him than he'd like to admit—*can't kid a kidder*, that's what someone said to me once. I had some of the dirty things inside of me too, like M. I could see how his eyes wouldn't clear, how he sometimes lost a beat between words. I imagined him working, getting every line perfectly straight, angling the nails in to not show. *Right here*, I wanted to tell him, *right up my side. You can't feel it, you can't see it, but there's a row of steel.*

I met M. on the street. Just walking by. He was. I was. I saw him coming, there at dusk. I stopped for him, his long legs, his hands jammed in his pockets, head tipped down to the pavement.

He stopped and said, "Hey."

I said, "Hello," and we walked along for a while, like we were already friends, like we were going the same way but not saying anything.

He said, "Are you following me?"

And I said, "Maybe."

"Good," he said. We kept going, and he added, "Follow me a little longer, and I'll buy you a drink."

I said, "Okay," and that was it. We walked around until it got too cold, and then we got trashed and went to my place. It was a good day, that one.

At first, M. was always coming around. I mean, I was inviting him and he was inviting himself and we liked it that way. I took him out, and once we took a little weekend trip up north, and we really did fuck a lot. I liked him because he got up early in the morning. I would make coffee, and M. would come rolling out of bed and into the kitchen. He claimed one of my cups, and we'd go to the window with the steaming coffee and drink it, and he would drink it to the bottom. I always threw the rest of mine out into the street, because M. had the window open, dragging on a rolly and having his morning space out. He was a remarkable beauty then, shirtless and still hot with sleep, stumbling on everything inside of him. I always wanted to lace my fingers into his and lead him back to bed and make him fit his body around mine, tongue in groove. Sometimes I did. And sometimes we'd just sit there until our cups were too cold to even pretend that we weren't done yet, and M.'s cigarette was smooshed out.

He said to me once, "Babe, I think I'm going to die." And I said, "I think you're wrong." I think for a minute he believed me, because then he said, "Fuck. That sucks," and we didn't really talk about his premonition anymore.

I woke up, and it was dark, as dark as stink, as dark as polished walnut. M. was there, but he was somewhere else too, curled up into himself and coughing, a cough that came right up from the bottom of him. He sounded like he would vomit or choke, but he didn't. He just kept hacking away at it; I think it wasn't even the cigarettes, that it was something else, some dead thing inside of him that wanted out. I put my hand on the small of his back, and he was still for a second before the coughing started again. I knew he was crying, because I swear I could smell the salt, and I wanted to run him a bath or press myself against him or say something sweet and profound that would make him stop, but I didn't. I lay in the dark with my hand there and M. shaking, and I whispered to him, "Shhh," like he was a child, but he didn't shush. *Measure twice, cut once*, I thought.

If only.

Sometimes in those days I got so tired, I could feel everything inside of me—blood vibrating along, my lungs empty and full and empty again. If I squinted my eyes, I could see M. coming toward me, his lank and his cuticles, as ragged as torn paper. And I really needed the sleep. I pulled myself up into a ball, and I arranged my blankets carefully around me. I thought nothing but perfect, serene thoughts, but it wouldn't touch me. It was the curse I had built for myself: a little house filled with nothing but a waking life. When all the joints were plumb and the rows neat, I wanted my eyes open to admire my own handiwork, to wait for M.'s fingers through the dark, to feel every kind of air on my skin. In those times I got up and went to the window and let the traffic sounds buzz through me, I made tea or sipped orange juice, and I didn't get angry about it. I thought if my worst problem was the red in my eyes, I was doing pretty good. I thought if M. were braver, he would have just fallen in love with me, and if I were braver, I'd have reminded him to be brave.

I thought of him with a handsaw and a hunk of oak. I thought of him with a brown bag of nails, with the bottom broken out and sharp silvers falling through the holes, leaving a trail so I could find him in the forest. And when I got there, where he was, in a clearing he had made, he'd be out there with a band saw and a stack of wet pine, beveling boards. I felt like I was late, because he'd already finished with the planer. There was a chain saw cooling on a stump, and he was sweating. I said, "Whatcha building, M.?" and he looked at the paper sack, soggy and empty at his feet, and said, "Hey."

He said, "How many nails did you find?"

I opened my palms to him, splotched crimson and white from the cold and from clutching so tight as to not drop even one. It was like my hands were platters, they'd grown so big, offering that chrome. M. studied the nails for a minute. He counted them, he picked through the pile, and threw out ones that were inexplicably bent, another that was missing a head. His machines were too quiet. I saw the long, orange extension cords, snaking to a power source that was out beyond the trees. He appraised me, he appraised the boards. He appraised the soft ground we were on and the part of his boot where the sole was tearing loose. "You tell me," he said, looking at the pile of wood he'd ripped through without planning. "You tell me."

M. and I got up one morning, an after-the-bar morning, and it was not two minutes before I saw there was something different.

"How'd you sleep?" I asked.

"Good," he said, but he was fidgeting and eyeing the coffee pot, which was percolating at the usual pace.

"Really," I said.

M. didn't answer me, he just keep watching the black drip into the glass, so I told him.

"You don't have to wait," I said. "It's okay."

He got up, and I wasn't surprised. He already had some saggy jeans on, and he managed to rustle up his filthy T-shirt and his jacket, jam a stocking cap on his head, and start getting gone out my door. I didn't kiss him good-bye, but I did turn off the coffee and go take a shower, and when I was sudsing my hair up with the lavender shampoo, I realized that I was sad that he left that way. It was the first time I wasn't sure if M. would be coming back.

There was this other problem—I mean besides M. and besides the sleep. I called it Danger On Stairs, but it could happen anywhere. Sometimes it was like the floor had been pulled out from underneath me or a chair suddenly tipped forward, but I hadn't moved and neither had the ground. I would plunge for a moment but without the weightless bliss. Usually, I was fine. The spin stopped, and I looked up, I looked around, and no one would have seen I'd been pitching. Only once, while I was in the kitchen, did I really fall; I was making pilaf, washing the rice and washing it again, while butter sizzled in a pan. I heard brass in my ear, all the way inside—trumpet, flügelhorn, I'm not sure—and the tap water smashing against the drain, and then I was on the linoleum. M. found the bruise on the back of my head, raised and probably purple, touched it like a jewel, just around the edges. *Where was your level?* I thought. *Your chalky blue string.* M. traced the tender spot through my hair and said nothing. He let his hand rest at my neck. He smelled like cedar, curlicued shavings. Really, what I wanted then was to get away from the window and lay down in the dark and have him take the cat's claw and pull out all the nails patching me together. I wanted to be rebuilt, holes puttied over and sanded smooth, but I didn't know how M. could do it, and he wasn't in restoration work anyway.

Instead I said, "Want another whiskey?"

And he said, "Please. No ice this time."

I brought him a clean glass part filled with a double shot, and he drank it immediately. He asked me if I would take off my shirt, and I did and stood before him, birch skin, gleaming white. I wondered if he knew that he was the wet one, the green one, the one who hadn't cracked yet.

He said, "Stand still," and I said, "I am still." Sometimes I couldn't tell. Maybe it was him seeing double or it was the world or I really was swaying to something. Like always, I just waited for it to go away, and just after I knew I was complete static, he said, "Better, girl, better."

After that morning when M. left me, I waited. I waited through one weekend and then another, and my bell was silent. I checked my telephone constantly, but he didn't call. I rang him up a couple of times, but there was no answer. I stopped leaving messages. I was sure he was home, and I was sure my voice on the machine cut through the quiet of his apartment like a saw. I spent a lot of time at the window, trying to see what M. had seen in the buildings. It was all a lot of glass to me. I was not impressed with the crossbeams or the height or the pattern made by the lights left on, the missing and broken teeth of the lights left out.

One night I went out with some girlfriends. I wasn't really looking for M., but I wouldn't have been opposed to running into him. In fact, I was a little surprised that I didn't, and I realized I had this idea that he was everywhere all the time, when of course he couldn't be. He was in one place, and I was in another. I swear I was wearing so much mascara, I could hardly keep my eyes open. At one point I tried to take some of it off in the bathroom but managed mostly to only pull out some eyelashes and smear black around my lids. Later, when my friends abandoned me or I them, I went home with a guy who was taller than even M. and very, very funny but sort of dopey and paunchy in a way I understood I didn't like, and I found that I couldn't even screw, because I was so dry. Packed full of sawdust, probably.

He didn't return. Ever. One day, though, I woke up, and I found I had actually woken *up*, instead of just groggily rolling to the side and opening my eyes. I hadn't solved much, the dizziness or what happened to M., but the break from insomnia was one damn precious blessing. I think how M. used to say that I wasn't much of an optimist, that I was definitely a glass-is-half-empty kind of gal, but he was wrong about me there. The difference between us was not how we understood halves. Maybe people who can build relate to it differently, something about their spatial thinking skills or something, but I think I didn't tell M. that what he didn't seem to be catching on to was the glass thing isn't real. The glass thing is supposed to trick us into believing half could be enough. I would like to tell him now. I would like to tell him, *I hope your back stays strong, and the light is good when you work*; I would like to tell him, *I dream you*, and usually I'm not even asleep. Mostly, though, I want to tell him that my optimism is not in question. I want to tell him that I understand the impulse to run, and I want to tell him, *No, really, don't believe that line about the glass*—take a full one or nothing at all.

The Car

When Brian's wife, Jenny, was first pregnant they went house hunting, leaving their efficiency condo in the city and venturing into the spiderweb of suburban living, looking for space and yards and wide, gleaming appliances. He had been surprised by her readiness to trade in her patent boots for plush carpeting, how mesmerized she was by the size of the developments and their pastoral names: Foxglove Run, Sage Hill, The Horizons at Rock Creek.

As their child transformed from pea to lima bean to lemon, Brian ran his fingers across slabs of granite countertop that were bigger than the entire bathroom of their condo. It takes only a drop of water cycling into ice to crack rock, but the finishes were glossy and smooth. The flecks of quartz sparkled. He wandered through the houses and tried to see Jenny brushing her brown hair in the master bath, or himself shaving at the sink. He thought of the little specks of razored-off whiskers that sometimes dotted the white cream, and how he was always very careful to get it all down the drain. He thought of how they had their toiletries organized in miniature tubs under the sink, of the early days when he had woken up and she was gone. He would stare at himself in the mirror and wonder if he'd done something wrong, if she was angry.

Married now, sometimes they fought, just as he had feared. They even fought when Jenny found out she was pregnant. He was drinking a beer and she had tossed the home test casually onto the coffee table.

"Two lines," she said. "Bingo."

He wasn't sure what it meant. "How many lines are there supposed to be?" he asked.

"Depends on what you're after," Jenny said.

"Okay," Brian said. He thought he was being even, measured. "What are we after?"

Jenny looked at him, frowning. He heard each bubble of carbonation in his beer fizzing.

When their friends asked them if they had been trying, Jenny said they weren't *trying* but they weren't doing anything to prevent it, either.

"We aren't?" Brian had wanted to know.

"Well, I'm not," Jenny said. "Have you been doing something? *I* was doing something, but *I* stopped."

He considered this. He had never asked about Jenny's birth control—not when they were dating, not now that they were spouses—it seemed secret and narcotic, something that wasn't his business. He couldn't tell if Jenny didn't care what he thought, or if she had done what he had done and not inquired.

One day Jenny had moved into the condo, and after this had gone on for a while, she had become his fiancée. They married in a small ceremony and her mother had gotten very drunk at the reception. It had been a nice night.

They'd only just celebrated their second anniversary and the kitchen was already a tangle of prenatal vitamins.

"I guess we need to move then," he said.

"I think we do," Jenny said. "Hopefully soon."

When they looked at houses, he imagined himself slogging through miles of commuter traffic with only the company of drive-time radio, and he felt a rift forming in the marriage. Brian also thought he and Jenny were arguing more lately—was it because she was hormonal and he was terrified? He found this explanation to be extremely likely. Before the pregnancy, if they had had heated words, one of them would take a walk to a local place and meet a friend, or read the paper, or have a slow cocktail at the counter. He liked how just a little separation, just the tiniest bit of distance, cooled them both. He liked how it was accomplished very easily, without a production. With every foot added to their prospective deck, he'd be farther and farther from the place where he could just step out for a few minutes, and then he would see himself, fuming, surrounded by the wide hallways and entryway arches of beige-y new construction, trapped by rows of fake wrought-iron fencing and hedge work.

In the middle of house hunting, he called his father. They had not been close for some time.

"Don't understand why you are renting anyway," his father said. "Just throwing away money."

Perhaps it was not a rift, just a little fissure.

When it came to real estate, his boss told him it was impossible to negotiate with a woman with child and so he (Brian) should skip the negotiations altogether and pick some boundaries, like not moving north of Park or south of Evans, and that even if they found the perfect home just a few blocks off, he should hold his ground and refuse to offer. Better yet, he should refuse to even look at it. Brian took a softer approach, and went to every showing Jenny was interested in. As their lowball offers were consistently declined, the clacking of their real estate agent's heels against concrete driveways faded to the smoosh of tennis shoes, and from pencil skirts and blazers to jeans and hoodies.

Jenny was not ill much but she was changing. Her belly was growing rapidly. She was more contemplative and more interested in cooking. For years, she hadn't done much in the kitchen besides heat water for coffee but now she left work early and Brian came home to full meals spilling off their tiny kitchen table and mounds of dishes like debris from a war zone. She took off her wedding ring, the ring she had chosen, and placed it on her jewelry tree where Brian figured it would hang indefinitely with all of the other things she might never wear again, like heavy necklaces of bright glass beads, chandelier earrings, and silver bracelets. When he asked her about the ring, Jenny said her hands were swollen, but Brian thought her fingers looked as slim as ever, perfect, in fact, as she plucked leaves off cilantro stems or cubed potatoes.

When their real estate agent told them she didn't want to work with them anymore, they both caved and put an acceptable offer on an acceptable three-bedroom ranch that was farther from the city than Brian liked and smaller and more used than Jenny had hoped for, and they moved in one weekend, packing up everything from their old life and watching the hired labor fill a truck.

It seemed so final to Brian. It seemed like they had so little.

He was surprised, almost, when all the boxes were unloaded into the new house that their contents were unchanged. It was almost as if by not breaking or spilling or getting lost or just vaporizing that his socks and records and thermal mugs were complicit in the move. Like they had agreed to the move and willed themselves to survive the transport, to be unpacked in a mortgaged space where neither he nor Jenny really wanted to live.

"I think this will be fine," Jenny said, after their first night in their new bedroom. "It feels okay. I forgot how nice the tile is in the shower."

"I'm glad you like it," Brian said.

"I didn't say I liked it," Jenny said. "I said I thought it would be fine."

On the weekend of the move, Jenny told Brian she had put in notice at work; she was already seven months pregnant and she didn't plan on going back. Brian suggested that they could carpool for the last few weeks and she could take her leave, and then decide. She said it was already done—no taking back a resignation now. He thought she might miss her job at the law office, where she was in accounting and which he thought she liked. The women had thrown her a shower, and the partners had given her a check inside a card signed by their admins. He thought she should have consulted him. She'd worked hard and was in a mid-level position, and before she was pregnant, she flashed wide smiles at parties and wore flowery, cleavage-baring shirts (a fact that he enjoyed, but people were often surprised by his wife).

"I think it makes more sense, anyway, that we are closer together in the day. What if the baby comes and I'm stuck in traffic," Brian said.

"I can call the ambulance," Jenny said.

Brian thought an ambulance seemed unnecessary, but he didn't say anything. At work—he was in sales—his boss had continued to remind him not to attempt negotiations. His boss had four children by three different wives. Brian did not aspire to be like him, but he could not deny that the man had more experience.

It was difficult and also ill-advised for Jenny to lift very much, so as they organized, Brian brought her boxes, opened them carefully, and then set them on a stool for easy reach. He was surprised at the quantity of packages that were directed to the baby's room—where had these things been hiding in the condo?

Jenny had decided they should wait to find out the sex, so the nursery had been painted a smooth, wasabi green. Every day when he was finally delivered from his commute, there were more parcels on the doorstep: a crib, which needed assembly, a stroller, which looked suitable for off-road terrain.

On the weekend they went shopping, in preparation. They purchased a bedroom set for the area Brian had hoped could be his office, but under Jenny's direction was becoming a guest room. He shrugged and swiped his Amex through the slot in the terminal. He accepted the receipt, folded it into smaller and smaller squares, and shoved it into his wallet. He arranged for delivery, and he followed his wife across the store's parking lot and into the next store, her belly a compass leading them through shop after shop, where he pushed the cart and she calculated. His feet hurt and he hated the plastic smell of the merchandise and he badly wanted a beer. She was frustrated with what she saw as the relative lack of gender-neutral clothing and wondered out loud why it was so impossible to make a few things in green or yellow.

"You wear blue," Brian said. "It's not only for men. I have a purple shirt you always say looks nice on me." The cart had one wobbly wheel and it squeaked on the waxed floor.

"It's not the same when they're little," she said. "I think I would feel weird."

"How many clothes does a baby need for one day, though?" Brian asked. The wheel protested.

"One day?" Jenny looked at him.

He heard his boss in his head. *No negotiation. No negotiar. Nich zu verhandeln.* "Yeah, I mean, by day one," Brian said, "we'll know if it's a boy or a girl. I'm saying how much green stuff do we really need, because pink and blue will be fine after that. Or any color."

"I don't think it will be fine, Brian," Jenny said.

"I think it will be fine," Brian said, and he wished they were not having this conversation in public.

"What if it's not fine?" Jenny said.

Brian pushed the cart around the corner. They were standing in a tall aisle of diapers shrink-wrapped into large bricks and he questioned how these could be realistically maneuvered into the trunk of the car.

"It will be fine." The skin around his lips felt dry. He wasn't really sure if they were talking about onesie colors or something else, but he wanted to be right. He wanted her to believe him.

The baby coming was very alarming to Brian. For months he had felt a knot in his belly—he speculated that maybe it was sympathy pains or indigestion, but he knew it was fear. He wondered if he should have prepared more, if he should not have fought Jenny so much on the house, because now he did not have an office. Now they had five times as much space as the condo, but they were running out of space anyway. He could admit there were some things that were nice about living out of the city center. Parking was nice. If they were going to have to do all this shopping, the proximity was nice. His commute was not nice, but it was not unbearable. On the drive home, he liked listening to a call-in radio show that offered advice to mostly women. Once he thought he heard Jenny's voice on the line— the program used a voice disguiser in some cases.

My husband is not excited for our baby, the caller said, her voice graveled through a machine. *I asked him if he wanted a boy or a girl and he said it didn't matter.*

Does it matter? the host asked.

No, said the caller. *Not to me. But I am surprised it doesn't matter to him.*

As it turned out, Brian was not in traffic when the baby came. He and Jenny were sitting on their sofa—a new sofa—on a Saturday morning and she gave a little grunt.

"Are you okay?" he asked, but she was already up, maneuvering away from the upholstery as her water broke, beautifully, he thought, all over her jammy pants and house slippers.

And then it was happening. He drove carefully to their new hospital, there was valet so he used that. The attendants brought a wheelchair for Jenny and she accepted it gracefully. There was some waiting, some paperwork. Mostly, from his perspective, waiting. When he went to Jenny in the room, she was in recline, and sweating. He had a hard time understanding it. Women had been having babies for thousands of years, but somehow the process had not sped up, unlike, say, intercontinental travel or building a fire. He wondered if there were some drugs the doctor should be using or if there was something Jenny should be doing differently—or something he should have done, like driven her to yoga classes. She had talked about yoga, but after he got out of the car at the end of the day, he was incapable of getting back in. He had told her to drive herself and she had given him a sad smile.

"It's *couples* yoga," she said, and the idea scared him enough that he went straightaway to take a shower.

After some more time passed, he was hungry and the hospital vending machine offered questionable granola bars and candy. He chose a Twix that was stale and demoralizing.

He was thinking of getting a new car. For as long as he had known Jenny, she had never had a car. He wasn't sure she should be at home all day with the baby and no car. He was also tired of running errands. As he waited, he thought about the car situation extensively. Jenny in the car, driving carefully with their baby. The child in the car, strapped in securely. The shine on the wheels, the new paneling. The gauges, glowing brightly against Jenny's cheeks and carefully illuminating the temperatures and pressures of the vehicle, in constant, quiet confirmation that everything was functioning normally.

It was hours later when their daughter came. Jenny gripped his hand—still, her fingers did not seem swollen—and Brian's thoughts went blank for a moment, as if he had gotten an electric shock or the wind knocked out of him, and when his head started firing again, he had a feeling like the time he successfully plunged out the garbage disposal and the pipes freed with a satisfying gurgle, and the knot in his stomach moved some.

They had a girl, tiny and new, with crumpled ears and gooey hair.

Jenny's face when she met their daughter—he had never seen anything like it.

He had to sanitize his hands and put on a gown over his rumpled clothes, but he held her while she screamed a perfect, whole sound.

"Hello," Brian said. "Your mother did very well, I think." He brushed his lips across her wrinkled forehead.

Her body was warm in his arms.

He thought that things were changing.

Jenny's mother came on the overnight flight and when she arrived she was angry at TSA and also everything else. Brian thought she had a ridiculous amount of luggage, but later recanted when he saw her packing included snacks and a large bottle of whiskey, which he would have picked up for her, and he told her so, but she said she wasn't sure if the store would have her brand. She had to have her brand.

They called their daughter Stella, which Brian had argued was a southern-sounding name or a kind of beer, but his mother-in-law's name was Lucy Estelle and Jenny told him it was Latin for *star*.

He was surprised at the baby's lull. He had taken time off work—his boss told him not to worry if he wanted to come back early, he wouldn't judge!—and had expected total chaos, but Jenny and her mother chatted in low voices and Lucy bleached the bathtub so Jenny could soak and, on day two, she cooked two huge pots of soup and two massive casseroles and divided everything up into labeled containers in the freezer. Stella mostly slept.

"Just in case," Lucy said, "you have a couple nights when all you can do is reheat." She winked and sipped from her whiskey. Brian went for a beer and clinked the neck of the bottle to the glass of rattly ice and liquor.

Brian had always thought his mother-in-law, in addition to being a drunk, was pushy, but he was grateful for her then, when Jenny was napping and Stella was fussing. She shoved his daughter into his arms and demanded that he change her or feed her from Jenny's pumped milk or walk in a circle and bounce her.

On night four, Brian woke to Lucy leaning over him—Jenny had been up every other time and was dozing deeply. Stella was screaming.

"Get up," something about the dark always urging a whisper, "and go to your daughter!"

"I'm up, I'm up," Brian said.

"She needs you," Lucy said.

Brian padded through the unlit house toward Stella, Lucy trailing with a blanket and a bottle. He knew she was training him for Jenny's sake; Brian didn't have younger siblings or young cousins, and his father had not been the hands-on type.

He liked that: *needs*.

He cradled his daughter's head with his hands.

When he had first met Jenny, they'd been at the show of a local band and he'd spilled beer all over her shoes. She was nice about it, though her friends were not—they sneered at him and told him he would have to buy her another pair. He was excited he would get to see her again. He had left Jenny with his number and said it was up to her, and the next day she called and said, *Nordstrom, daddy-o*, and he picked her up in front of her building and they hung out in the mall like teenagers might have.

She chose a pair of suede platforms but, when he was checking out, confessed her shoes from the other night had been from Payless.

"That's okay," he said. "Should we go somewhere else?"

They spent the afternoon on a coffee-shop patio until finally Jenny said that she really wanted to get going so she could try on her new shoes. When Brian said he would drop her home, she said no. *Your place.*

Brian did get a new car, while Lucy was still in town. He chose a cherry-red sedan and he fully admitted that his salesman training had dissolved when he thought of his daughter. He had been completely upsold on safety features. The interior was gray, and he felt it was extremely sharp. He asked for one of those large bows that he had seen on television, but the dealership told him they only had those in winter and they were extra anyway.

He told the man who was helping him that the car was for his wife, who was at home with their daughter. The man told Brian that if it were him, he would give the old car to his wife and keep the new one.

"Kids, you know," he said. "They make a lot of messes."

"I'd rather have her in the newer one," Brian said. "More reliable."

"But that upholstery will show everything, man. Just wait."

"Okay," Brian said. He was all right with waiting.

After the financing was sorted and the signatures collected, Brian understood he had no way to get the cars back without Lucy or Jenny, so he gave the man another fifty dollars from his wallet to follow in the old sedan and one of the maintenance staff followed them both.

He liked his life, he decided. He liked the women: Lucy, Jenny, Stella. He kept his radio silent and he repeated their names as he drove. The car was smooth against the pavement, and the wheel responded to even the slightest touch. Brian thought they were a little like the pioneers then, the three men and his two cars, caravanning across an unfamiliar landscape, headed toward a new idea of home.

There and Back

The motel is on the edge of town, surrounded by brushy hills and other motels, in sight of the Spokane stretch of Interstate 90. The numbers ascend one through fifty, but there are only twenty-five rooms, each door marked with odds. Inside there is thick potato-brown carpet, and on a good day Constance finds the outline of a foot that has sunk into the shag, the print carefully left behind. She likes this evidence of occupation.

The owner hired her just off the bus and let her sleep in an empty cot for three days until she found somewhere to go—before she found David, a remote acquaintance, a friend of her cousin's. Her cousin said to leave a note for him at the Handi-Mart on First and she did. Now she stays in David's small apartment in exchange for a little of her money. She is paid in cash, a stack of twenties as thin and stiff as the starched coverlets swathed on each bed.

She stocks the bathroom with cakes of tiny soap and runs the vacuum; changes the sheets whether they've been slept in or not. On gray mornings the neon from the sign, Sleepy Sage Motel, flashes pink into numbers seven and nine. She empties the little, round garbage cans and puts in clean bags; rubs cup rings out of the blond, wood dressers.

The fact that the Earth orbits the sun has not left her mind since the end of June. She knew when the heat had hit, was there to stay, and she thought of the planet circling; she thought of the light coming stronger down onto her, noticed how the difference in outside temperature made everything more immediate. Her pores felt closed up, holding her own heat inside. She was aware of the room, number five—the constant buzzing of the mini fridge, the peachy mold in the bathroom. It was a kind of relief.

The cleaning is welcome work. It is a disappearing act. Pillows puffed to erase the indentation of a head, the first square of bathroom tissue folded to make it appear unused. She has a cart and Nora, the owner, carefully rations supplies onto it from a locked cabinet behind the front desk. She says things like, "You shouldn't be out of shampoo yet, unless you're taking it home." Nora does all the things a woman in her position is supposed to, like constantly reapplying pearly lipstick and smoking her thin cigarettes down to a nub.

It is rare that Constance sees a guest. They arrive in the evenings and are gone when she opens the doors with the master key. They leave behind little and most of it useless—single earrings and socks, gum wrappers and full ashtrays. Loose change sometimes, on the nightstand, hair on the rim of the sink. Almost always, though, there is some kind of smell: pizza and perfume; burnt tobacco; that kind of shoes-on, panties-pushed-aside sex.

At home—the home she is borrowing—Constance has seen quickly that her roommate, David, is the restless kind. He is in and out of the apartment, always with a pack strapped to his back. The pack is big, green. He leans it up against the wall.

The apartment is furnished only with scavenged things, and she pretends the signs of wear belong to her. Poorly ventilated, with seriously chipping paint, it is spread with decaying plaster that makes a fine dust for her to sweep as it flakes off the walls. Occasionally the plaster comes down in sizable chunks, and she has taped pretty pieces of fabric and interesting magazine ads over the scars. Sometimes she hopes for the building to be condemned and torn down, and she imagines herself sitting at the window—she would refuse to move; she would have principles—until the last climactic moment, when the wrecking ball swung through the glass and pummeled her head, knocking her to the ground as the building collapsed in on itself, falling to a heap of brick and old bathtubs.

David is not home often, but Constance can always tell if he is inside, even before the door is halfway open—there is a different kind of quiet, stillness when he's not, and the backpack that she doesn't open or ask about.

One day she comes home after work, and he says, "Jesus. You're bright red."

Agreeing, she looks at her sunburn. She is sore but not unhappy—the color is even and smooth.

Since she has seen him last, she has been up to the roof of the building. Sometimes he is gone for days and she doesn't mind. But she went up to the roof and found a place that was silver with early sun and sat down, careful not to land on anything sharp. It was all a surprise to her—her new home with a strange man and this new life that she came to with her skin white as a bride.

She could not say, in clear terms, exactly what she was doing up there. She wanted something specific and she stripped her clothes and soaked in the sun, thinking there might be precision with the pink.

When she thinks about David, Constance remembers in school when she'd ride around with boys and let them lie on her and fuck her because she saw no reason not to. Saw them in a series of next days when they would not look at her, and she eyed them right in the face.

Even after he notices her burn, she keeps hiking the seven flights to the roof of their building and letting the sun touch her hard. It gives her awareness of her body. But she is careful to avoid blisters, and she feels like she has control of something, though her skin breaks out, aggravated by light.

Then there is the day that she hears the roof door open, and she reaches quick for her clothing. Steps crunch across the debris, and she slides into the shade of a metal-sided outlet. David walks to the edge of the roof, leans over, spits, looks around a little, and heads back to the door.

When she is not at the Sleepy Sage or with David, all she can think about is being out of the city. Constance dreams of her father and of his chores, like cutting hay and spreading manure through the garden, tilling so it's mixed. She has this feeling where she is not sure if she is moving on from another life or if it has moved on from her.

The day David almost catches her on the roof, she calls her father from a pay phone and asks him to describe the smell of the alfalfa fields. He says they smell like they always do, and that is a comfort to her, that it hasn't changed, but also bothersome because she can't remember what *always* smells like.

Living with her father, she had grown up poor and, for much of her life, had not known it. Her mother was gone since she could remember. Maybe her father knew where but he didn't say. Constance liked to speculate: maybe she was living quietly on the edge of a canyon in a pretty house with good insulation; but more likely, thought Constance, her mother was scraping by like the rest of them, as a clerk or the kind of itinerant prostitute she herself was determined not to become, happy, still, to be away from the chicken shit and hog feed. Or unhappy and too proud to come back or lost in a maze of hitched rides on boxcars and truck beds. Maybe plain dead.

When she was young Constance's father had put her on the two-hour bus ride with all the other rural kids and sent her to school in a blue, pleated skirt, a plaid blouse, and a pair of tennis shoes, with her cotton tights. As she grew she switched to filmy jeans, patched and repatched. She learned to sew, but sloppily, on the old treadle Singer her mother had left behind, and made herself shirts with crooked seams and bunched sleeves. She mended her father's pants and replaced the buttons on the fronts of his flannels when they popped off: first, she took the button from the very top of the collar, because he didn't ever use it; then she moved the ones from the front pocket, since she had never known him to fasten those either. Sometimes there was a spare on the inside seam.

Her father had been distressed when she told him that it was time for her to go.

He had extolled the better parts of their life together: the coffee after dinner; cigarettes rolled from bags of shaggy tobacco when the evening chores were done; the clear light of morning in the country; little bits of dirt in the teeth from garden vegetables. He reminded her summer was coming, and they could swim in the irrigation pond, they could train the raspberry canes so the rows would grow together and make a tunnel down the center, and Constance could lie in it, back to dirt, face to sky, smell of berries around her, water from the drip lines laced through the stalks, misting down around her. There would be rhubarb cobbler and fresh lettuce.

But because he could not say that he needed her to stay—for company, for affection—she was ready to go. She was ready to go anyway, with the old suitcase and the little dab of cash he offered and she was reluctant to take, though soon glad she did. There was no bus depot in their town, only a scheduled stop on the side of the road near a gas station that had gone through three different owners in Constance's time alone, and she kept hoping he might give her some reason not to climb on the Greyhound.

"Don't end up like your mother," her father said.

"How's that?" she asked. "How'd she end up? I don't know."

"I don't know either. That's what I don't want."

"Sure," Constance said. She promised. She stepped on the bus. The smell of oil and gasoline was strong.

As it pulled away she looked back from the bus until she couldn't see him. Already she was cramped in the seat and crying and glad that she didn't have too much luggage. Most of her things were under her seat, within reach; *I can decide*, she thought, *to jump off at any stop and hike home.*

The longer she is away, the more significant her leaving is to her. It grows in her memory and changes, and she wonders if it moves in her father's head as well, until the actual moment when the bus pulled away is overshadowed by their recollections of it, until the moment itself is nothing.

Constance pulls the vacuum in long parallel lines across the carpets, wipes her rag in straight strokes. Her body is changing, forgetting the movements of her and her father's house, learning this other place. A steady ache in her wrists, a sting in her back. Sometimes, when she's behind the rooms taking a break, she shakes out her hands and tries to stretch a little, bends over and touches her toes, vertebrae cracking like corn popping on the way to her shoes.

In number forty-one there is a shoelace that winds around the brush for the vacuum and jams it. She tips her head into number eleven's kitchenette sink, mouth beneath the faucet, and drinks and drinks, trying to keep hydrated. She can think about nothing but going back to the apartment, nothing but escaping the waxy lemon furniture polish and twists of other people's hair tangled in the shag. When she exits the room, pushing her cart along the pitted concrete sidewalk in front of the doorways, she sees a bobby pin wedged into a crack in the kitchenette counter.

When she has left for the day and is heading for home, the heat is like walking through a wall. The city is dirtier and softer, the asphalt and concrete, rubber and glass, neon all on the verge of liquid, wavy distortion from the fumes of the gas stations. The exhaust and oil and industrial smoke is bitter and, under the force of the sun, even less like something that resembles breathable air.

She keeps walking; there is not much else to do. David is in the apartment when she reaches it, and she heads straight for the bathroom and collapses on the floor. She slides across the linoleum until her shoe's soles are flat against the tub and her back against the wall, sweat and the beginning of tears pooling around her, and she feels like she is spinning. It is like the room does not know she is trying to be still and cool, as if the heat is in collusion with the room.

She climbs into the bath to cool down, cold water across her tender skin.

David collects and he pack-rats. One day she sees lightbulbs in a row on the floor. He has one that is like a soap bubble, perfectly round and opalescent. He takes a tiny bulb out of a taillight and a monstrous flood lamp from the front of a garage. There's one that's vaguely flame-shaped out of a cheap lobby chandelier and a short piece of fluorescent tubing.

He tells her about looking for gaslights in the pawnshops but doesn't find anything worth having. He is taken with variations in shape, size, function, wattage. Out loud she says it is a nice little collection, good selection, but worries about misstepping and crushing glass beneath her feet.

She sees him in everything. They go to a second-run movie house, and the slope of the theater armrest is the curve of his spine; the way the lightbulbs bow out at the thickest part is like the space he keeps around himself—the distance from the filament, the center, relatively small but essential.

And she watches him as he sleeps. His face pinches and the lumps of his irises flit beneath his lids when he is in deep dreaming. She likes the look of his ratty hair and sebaceous oil on his skin. He is a still, quiet sleeper. He is like a vine under the sheets; so thin, the covers are hardly disturbed.

Toward the end of the month, Constance has a little money left, and they go out for groceries. Climbing the flights of stairs back to the apartment, she listens to him, though it seems like he is giving her more of a confession than a conversation.

What he says about it is what she expects: metal and bulletproof glass; doors that lock in electronic synchronization. He cannot say much about visitors—the few fathers, mothers, siblings, children, family, but mostly women in papery layers of powder and mascara who had nothing better to do than offer themselves to men whose location, whose devotion, they could be sure of for a year or years. He didn't have visitors. Bored and depressed, closed in by concrete.

"It must have been little things adding up. Like collecting pennies. They're nothing until you make a roll. I got fifty and was popped," he says.

"Well, you must have done something," Constance says.

He looks her straight in the face. "You're right. It's boring, petty stuff, some houses up on Perry, but I had a record as a juvenile."

"A delinquent," she says.

"That's right. You okay with that?"

"Yes," she says. She means it.

He goes on to tell her that it was impossible to live without weather, and when he went outside, he'd try to soak it all in: sun, rain, wind, rotten leaves on the sidewalks, and sleet. In prison he got sores in his mouth because the food was acidic, the sleep poor, and the food heavy. When he was released he had a few things: his wallet, which was mostly intact, the clothes he'd originally been arrested in, another set that was state-issued, and his walking money. And he tells her how he'd been adept at spotting loneliness—he'd been surrounded by it as much as fencing and concertina wire. So much so, he says, he thinks he'll be able to recognize the ache of isolation for the rest of his life.

She does not ask if he sees loneliness in her. When he is done they put the groceries away.

Constance is worried and she wonders about her father. For a moment she believes she could sit on the porch of the house— no, up in the attic—as long as it took until he would just talk to her, even if her hair grew down the stairwell and out the front door, her head like an old, mushy onion rotting from the inside, skin translucent and sheeting off around her, teeth dropping on the floor like a split jeweler's box of topaz.

Then David comes home late when she has two days off coming and says, "Do you know how to drive?"

"Of course," she says.

He is standing close to her, and she feels something slide into her hand. A set of keys. She is quiet, though what she intends to say is *dangerous.*

"How'd you get it?"

He shrugs. He smiles. "It has a full tank."

David does not want to leave the car parked in the street overnight, but she convinces him it is okay, and they decide to get up early in the morning. She makes coffee for the road and puts hers in a jam jar.

As they drive the asphalt appears smoother and blacker than she remembers it. Since she has come to Spokane, she hasn't been in a car, and, at times, the speed and the way she is in absolute control of the vehicle is remarkable, entirely unlike being on foot, and she is pleased with the rediscovered sensation. It is not a particularly fancy car—a two-door American model. David tells her that he plans on dumping it within a couple of days, someplace where it will be found quickly. Once they get out of Spokane County they switch drivers, and the more time he spends behind the wheel, the more comfortable he seems, and he gradually taps the accelerator down closer to the floor.

They roll by the farmlands and small towns, and Constance mostly looks forward. She's drawn out of trying to predict the next slight corner or dip in the road by his sudden slowing of the car. He makes a sharp turn up a short driveway that she can see to the end of; there's an imitation farmhouse, like many, close to the road. It's built with modern vinyl siding and pressboard, though the basic architecture is similar to that of early twentieth-century agricultural homes.

"It looks sort of empty, doesn't it?" he asks and stops the car when the driveway opens up to the yard and some gravel in front of the garage. "I bet if there's someone here, they'll come out in a minute or two."

"Yeah, probably." She looks out the window. The yard is wide and very green in some places, brittle brown in others. There's a swing set a few steps from the front porch, and the plastic seats are faded and cracked from the sun.

"No one yet," he says after a minute.

"Nope," she replies, uncomfortable.

He starts the engine of the car, and she hopes he's going to drive away. Instead, he turns up the air-conditioning. "That feels good," he says.

"Yeah," she says, because it does.

"Okay." He shuts off the car and opens his door. Constance follows. "I'll knock," David says, "to be sure." He climbs the five steps to the door and teeters a little on the last one, having slightly lost his balance. Looking back at her, he smiles and raises a fist to the screen. They wait. No one. David tries the handle but it's locked. "That's a good sign," he says and turns to descend the five steps.

At the rear of the house, he reaches for the knob of the back door, and it does not turn. Picking up a plastic dump truck that's overturned in a weedy flower bed, he breaks out two panes of glass and reaches his arm in to undo the lock. She hears the *click* of the bolt coming undone, and they proceed through a messy mudroom.

Inside the decor reminds her of nothing. Cream walls. Beige carpet.

They make their way through the house, opening drawers and peeking into closets. Snooping seems harmless and she likes it.

"There's nothing in here," he says. He is at the bureau in the master bedroom, fingering some cheap jewelry and the ceramic, heart-shaped container that holds it—tangled necklaces, rings for a wide finger. On the other side of the room, he pulls a drawer all the way out of the dresser and dumps it on the water bed as Constance flicks on the light in the adjacent bathroom, looks around, and goes back to observing David. He paws through the mess of men's hankies and unmatched socks. Finding nothing, he leaves the whole mess wadded there, the water bed bucking.

She follows him throughout the house. He reaches above the couch and slaps the floral-and-straw arrangement hanging askew on the wall; the silk flowers and huge cotton bow tip sideways. He overturns the wide, plush couch and snorts at the wisps of webby dirt and bits of previously unreachable gravel missed by the vacuum.

"I'm going to the kitchen," Constance says.

David stares at the recliner, then turns it so it is upside down and facing the wall.

In the kitchen she makes four sandwiches—two with peanut butter and two with cold cuts—and finds a thermos to fill with milk. She leaves what's left of the gallon container—a half of a cup or so—out on the counter. This, it seems to her, is the worst she personally is capable of doing. The utensils she's used go in the dishwasher, and seeing that is hasn't been run, she starts the cycle.

"Let's get out of here," David says as he ambles into the kitchen.

Constance finishes packing the sandwiches in waxed paper. She walks back to the master bedroom and into the bathroom, leaves the door open, and she can see the mess he's left on the bed. For a minute she contemplates cleaning it up and putting the living room back together, wondering which would be worse: returning home with the suspicion someone had been inside—the couch and recliner back where they belong but slightly off-kilter, the missing bread, clean dishes—or knowing, unequivocally, instantly upon opening the door. She remembers the broken windows, irreversible evidence, and decides to leave the house the way it is.

It is about three more hours' drive. At a rest stop they chew the meat sandwiches and drink the milk. When they arrive at her father's house, Constance is impressed by how easily the car has covered the distance.

Already she can tell that something is not right. His truck is not there. The lawn is tipped in brown, and all the flower beds look peaked. Around the back the garden is stunted and being taken over by weeds that can handle the heat without irrigation. There are some rows in the garden only half dug, as if they were deserted mid-planting, and others in half bloom. She can tell much of the neglect is irreparable in this season. Inside, the garbage can is empty except for a fresh bag; there is not a single dish in the sink. The icebox has been cleaned of everything. She peeks in her father's room and sees that it looks cleaner than usual. Her room is absolutely the way she left it. There is nothing, as far as she can tell, to indicate where he has gone or why, though she thinks he must have planned the departure, because he tidied.

David is given the tour of the house, and it is not much—the two downstairs bedrooms, the kitchen, pantry, a little living room, a tiny dining area. The upstairs is decent-sized, enough for more rooms, but the whole space is used like an attic and is entirely unfinished. The sheets of gypsum board are exposed and the floor rough. There are boxes of papers and old clothes, beat-up furniture, a few little windows that don't open. Constance thinks that the things here are all very usual—not a single treasure, no heirlooms, no tableware locked in velvet-lined cases or heavy jewelry or anything but a bunch of junk, distinguishable from other people's junk only because she recognizes it. She leafs through some papers, half expecting a flash of recollection or at least a pang of curiosity, but there is only dust and a dry, pulpy smell.

"I guess we go back now," she says to David.

"Want to spend the night and see if he comes in the morning?"

"I think it's going to be longer than that."

"I'd like to stay." He looks at her.

"All right," she says.

David goes down the stairs, but she does not follow him. There is nothing on the second floor Constance hasn't seen a hundred times before; she probably carried half of it up herself. She remembers, as a girl, climbing the stairs and hoping, when she reached the top, she'd find something new. A fat envelope with foreign-looking postage from her mother or a portfolio of important, revealing documents that her father, in his haste, forgot to hide, but, always, it was the same, and the tracks in the dust were only hers from the time before.

Downstairs and out in the yard, she gets in the grass under the shade of the Russian olive with the ants and the aphids. She can see the underside of the tree's leaves, see all the little bugs that crawl across her arms. She sprawls out, does not know if she is becoming nostalgic for her girlhood or just for this place, the house with its smell of old, lived-in wood, well water, and smoke, the yard that is dying now, and the quiet that is coming with the falling dusk, only her own breath audible. Getting up, she walks down the hill that leads to the barn and the pens. There is still hay stacked in the lower section, and mice dart out, startled, when she kicks at the bales, but the coop and the pigsty are empty. The watering trough for the cow looks like it has been dry for weeks, so if the cows had been left behind, they'd be dead from dehydration by now—for a beast of that size, it only takes a day. It's obvious to her that her father is gone for a long time—maybe for good.

She climbs the ladder to the top part of the barn, the hayloft, and lies out on a section of bales. It has an open space all around it, near the roof, for ventilation. There are birds living in the eaves and shitting in the rafters. It gets darker. Finally, she decides to look for David and finds him crouched on the porch steps. She has hay in her hair.

"I'm watching the sun go," he says.

She shrugs. "Yeah?"

"You don't like sunsets?" he asks.

"Sometimes it seems like every one looks the same." She opens the screen door, walks inside, and makes a round through the house, double-checking everything. There is no power—not a surprise because the electricity was always a little sporadic— and so when she lifts the tap handle, there isn't any water, not even a drip. If he drained the pipes, she thinks, it means he's gone through the winter. The phone, installed in one of her father's fits of worry for impending old age ("Emergencies!" he said to her), is dead.

She finds her sleeping bag, crammed in her bedroom closet, and tears the blankets off her father's mattress. She makes two separate beds, close together, on the grass outside. Though he is reluctant to leave his spot on the porch, before it is too dark, she takes David down the trail, toward the barn, to show him where the outhouse is, which smells strong from the heat of summer. The house is only partially plumbed, and this is one of the ways, much like her father, and she thinks sometimes herself, it straddles two times.

In the new dark she climbs into her sleeping bag, wiggles out of her pants, and piles them on top of her shoes.

"I'm sorry about the ants. We don't put out poison. They're just the little black kind that don't bite," she says.

David lights a cigarette he has rolled from a tiny pouch of tobacco. "Okay," he says.

As it gets darker the stars become more apparent, a gauzy net of light in the loom of the sky. She hears him crawl into his bed and root around a little, trying to get comfortable. The yard is slightly sloped, but she knows she's picked the flattest part of it, because she's slept outside so many summers.

In the morning she wakes early because her head is cold. She takes her things inside. David, sleeping, looks better than she has seen him in weeks, and she thinks it must be from the air. There is a manual draw for the well near the garden and she fills a quart jar from the spigot and takes it to where he is sleeping. She has drunk half the water and had one of the remaining sandwiches by the time he wakes.

"Pick up your stuff," she says. "We should get going. Water?" she asks, extending her arm.

He shakes his head. "No, thank you."

They decide to leave the car on the outskirts of the city. They've both become a little nervous in the shiny, black machinery surrounded by upholstery and green dash lights. Constance feels like she can't escape the petroleum—plastic and gas, rubber and paint. David pulls all the way off the road, where it's in no danger of being hit, props the hood open, and turns on the flashers. He locks the keys inside. She asks if he thinks the dregs of milk from the thermos will stink it up, but he doesn't answer.

They run for a while, putting a good distance between themselves and the vehicle, and then walk. The day is cool and by the time they get to the first stoplight, Constance has a sense of displacement. She is not ready to go back to her work at the hotel but not ready to abandon it altogether. She is concerned that her father has vanished, but she also understands it. She thinks that her family—her mother she does not know, her father whom she knows too well—must have come from the kind of people who know inherently how to walk on sand and not leave a footprint. Or who lean away from the light, who stay in a patch of shadow, where no one really sees them.

After being away from the metered lights and measured sectioning of the city, she is in a position to notice the strangeness, the noise, and the way there is a low glow that hovers over everything. She wonders if there is a perfect patch of darkness in the entire place.

The House

As a younger woman, before I met my husband, Julian, and even through our first few years, especially before our daughter, I enjoyed drinking to excess. To begin with, I loved the color of booze. Amber and smoke and burnt cherry. There were many mornings where I was left befuddled over what had happened the night before, and I would lie in my bed with my quilts cocooned around me and parse back through what I could remember.

This made for a long, slow waking up and gave the day a kind of dimness that I felt now. Though the pieces were all there, I was not sure of the pattern.

And even more than that, I was unsure of the point.

We had a pretty home. We had chosen all the tasteful colors. Mint, robin's egg blue, fresh cream. It was the kind of home that always had enough clean linens and blankets and pillows for guests, always a decent bottle of wine in the pantry. There were many windows and sun, when there was some, streamed into every room. We lived in Seattle's Jackson Park, close to the city center, an older neighborhood. It was a home I had baked bread from scratch in, a home with a big stereo and a small television, waxy refinished hardwood floors.

And lately I felt filth everywhere.

I'd lost my job. I had been working in the registrar's office at the University of Seattle, matching requirements to credits earned and filling requests to have sealed copies mailed to important companies and graduate schools and occasionally to the students directly. Then the perpetual budget crises. Every fiscal quarter my duties changed, as the deans rearranged the staff to maximize efficiency, to reduce the number of salaries paid. When I was laid off, I thought I might go back, but as the days stretched into weeks, I realized I didn't want to. Julian, half partner in a consulting firm he'd started with a college friend, was starting to make real money. Our daughter, Anne, came home from kindergarten for summer vacation and I distracted myself with epic sessions of dress up and make-believe. That was the blessing of having a girl. When the holidays ended I was still unemployed. I wasn't really looking. After the university politicking, I was not ready for Seattle's vicious job market.

Then, as Anne went back to school, all I had was the house.

It wasn't that Julian and I didn't keep things clean before. It was more like I was looking for something in the cracks, in the rafters.

I took it apart, put it back together. Every closet, every drawer, every envelope filled with scraps of paper or rubber bands; I opened everything, sorted it, closed it up. Even, I pried the molding from around the bathroom floor—you wouldn't believe what's behind there, lint and pubic hair and a few tiny spiders— and wiped it clean, tacked it back to the wall with invisible finishing nails.

I thought of my daughter. She was plowing through first grade, and I had missed her birthday in early September. I just wasn't aware of the days. Julian had told me, of course, but "next Wednesday" didn't mean much to me then.

I loved her, but I hadn't wanted her all the time. I remember the night I got pregnant. I had known it would happen. Julian and I had been married almost a year, and we'd been recently discussing children. I was drunk again and on our walk home from the local pub I saw, through a street-level window, the last moments of a 30-something party. I was twenty-seven. Parents had scooped up their toddlers from where they'd been napping on the couches or back bedrooms, and at least half the people had a sleepy child in their arms. I knew these people would buckle up, that no one would drive home too loaded, that if they had nasty things to say to each other they'd save it for another day. The children had turned these ordinary people decent, and I wanted it.

And I told Julian.

And it took one time.

I had been off of my birth control for months. Even that early on, we were rarely having sex, and even if we did, neither of us could come, so Julian, at some point, would give up and plod into the bathroom and finish himself off, and I would wait in the dark bed, and wonder what was going on with us, and in the morning before work, after he was gone, I would masturbate while I thought of nothing.

So when I told Julian what I had seen at the party, he came at me with a passion I hadn't seen in him since our wedding night. With a passion I thought we both had given up.

And I didn't know how to tell him it had all been a mistake. Not a mistake. A misunderstanding.

And here was Anne, seven now, even if I had forgotten, our daughter and quieter than her father or me, spilling vials of glitter onto glue and drawing on scraps, decorating her room with cutouts of pretty paper she salvaged from the trash. She had an eye for it, I could see, angling her homemade stencils to pull a star or flower or half of a letter from a package of almond soap or a sack from the gourmet markets where Julian shopped.

It was the effort he made for me, shopping. We had always had fresh vegetables and interesting fruits: quince and pomegranate, Asian pears.

What I can say for Julian: he gave me anything I wanted.

That's the way marriage goes sometimes, I suppose. As our friends around us paired and coupled off, I would say, *Congratulations.* I would say, *I hope this is exactly what you want.* But you can't know, ever, until the marriage is happening, and by then, you've already battened down every available hatch. The blood has been drawn, the results filed. You've been witnessed to have pledged yourself.

I liked Julian. He was great sometimes. We did still talk, about Anne, or politics, or the finer points of sedimentology—he'd studied to be a geologist when he was in college. We talked about public policy. We talked about any number of things that some ordinary lives never touch on.

We didn't talk about why, after a few tousles around the time Anne was conceived, we'd stopped having sex again. We didn't talk about why we were talking about the natural and social sciences instead of the way we spiraled inward. We didn't talk about the way that if we didn't read the paper or get a nice dose of CNN we'd have nothing, really, to discuss.

It was easy, though, to avoid any real topics. Relationships, I had come to think, were like that: like the edible parts of a snail. Sort of squishy in the same way a full bag of kitchen garbage is—soft and sweetly, slowly spoiling. But perfect it—rip out the innards, purge the guts, and pour it all back into the shell—and it's coveted gourmet. It's stylish and satisfying. It's butter and magic.

Julian and I, though, we liked our hiding places just as much as any in the molluscan class, so I can't blame him for the fact we would talk heliciculture before we'd talk about our insides.

I can't say I had no idea how badly, even if I clung to the house, I wanted to be away from him and what I had come to think of as The Marriage. Sometimes I would look at him and think, *Christ, why are you here?* His shoulders, when he'd be at the kitchen counter, doing something like normal, like grinding coffee, seemed so ridiculously enormous, like two wheel wells.

When I'd first met him, I'd loved his big hands and broad fingers. He cupped my face in a very particular way—tips of his fingers behind my ears and his palm on my chin, supporting my head like one might with an infant. But as time went on, his touch was less endearing. The second time we stopped being intimate nearly altogether, I went through a period where if we were in our bed and he reached to touch me I would say, "Julian, did you wash your hands?"

Sometimes, he would roll over, toss back the covers, and slip into the bathroom. I'd hear the water on and the splashing while he soaped up. He would come back to me with his nails neat and his skin smooth, touched with the smell of my almond soap. And sometimes he would pull back from me, turn, and go to sleep.

Thing was, I didn't care how it turned out either way as long as I didn't have his dirty paw between my legs.

After Anne went back to school, one day I picked out an iron on the internet, printed out the product information for him, left it on the kitchen table. The next evening, when he came home, there was the box, a perfect rectangle with a shining triangle inside. This marked the start of a new phase. My phase of steel.

Sometime, while I was muddling around with Anne, I'd jammed my ring finger. I kind of pretended it was broken, though I refused to see a physician. That would mean leaving the house. So, Julian brought home a brace, aluminum curved over blue foam, and I wore it. I was still wearing it, months later. I took it off every day, washed, and put it back on. I wore this instead of my wedding band.

I liked to click it against metal stair railings, against glass. I waited for Julian to tell me to stop. Nervous sounds, like drumming fingers, drove him mad. He said nothing. I tapped out the beat of any song I could think of. To him it must have been the same series of *clink clink clink* on the ceramic countertops, but I heard saz, I heard drums.

I told Julian he didn't need to send his shirts out anymore, now that I had this miraculous iron.

"Miraculous?" he said to me from where he stood in the kitchen.

"It's engineering," I said. I thought I sounded delightfully coy and I shook the ice in my cocktail.

And I was right. I tapped my brace against the slick of the iron, and Julian's shirts were as crisp as origami paper, our cotton sheets as smooth as Anne's skin. I had never had an iron like this, puffing steam as thick as cigar smoke.

I also continued to do the usual things—wash the sugar bowl and defrost the freezer. I hosed off the upper and the lower deck.

It was fall by then and the yard needed tending. I'd done nothing with it all summer. Back when I lost my job, I had at first been ambitious but then managed to miss the earliest annuals, and since they hadn't all summer, I wondered if my irises would bloom ever again, but I didn't cross onto the lawn. Really, past the deck, I didn't go outside.

I held my iron like a weapon.

I ordered Middle Eastern cookbooks and supplies: cardamom and special ground red peppers; a string of cleaned, dried sheep intestines; pressure pots and Syrian tea. I was keeping myself busy.

I felt like I was grieving and I thought maybe I could just move through the stages of grief. I knew them from a few years of therapy in my early twenties, before I met Julian. I thought, *denial, anger, bargaining, depression, acceptance*, why not.

The cookbooks were helpful. I prepared vast pots of rice and garbanzo beans, warm garlicky yogurt and any kind of lamb. Peppers drowned in oil and tomato. I served Julian olives and goat cheese for breakfast, made him strong tea. I made the cups sing with my metal brace and he said nothing.

I marveled at cooking. Follow the directions and it's perfect every time.

On weekdays, at three in the afternoon, Anne arrived home from school and I started dinner.

I still, after all the years she'd been with us, could not see my face in hers.

I had tried. I had studied myself in the mirror, my straight, light brown hair, my wide, freckled nose. Her legs, her arms, the way she bent her elbows, she seemed to belong entirely to herself.

I liked it when Anne was home; if I could describe myself as ever missing anyone, it was her. She was still a quiet child. Contained. Average sized for her age, not particularly pretty, but there was sharpness in her hazel eyes. The color she had gotten from her father, but that look, I thought, that look like *You don't have to tell me twice* or *I am not amenable to these constant interruptions* or *Can you see the way the light made this shadow?* certainly came from me.

Thoughtfully, once she stepped off the bus, walked the block and a half from her stop, she would pause on our porch and pull off the notes my mother had left there during the day. My parents lived nearby. If there was a package I had not retrieved and it was not too heavy, she would drag it in the door.

She would say, without fail, "Mom! I brought in the deliveryables."

I didn't know where she had heard this word or how it had gotten twisted for her. I didn't know where she had learned these types of tiny kindnesses. I didn't know who taught her to lock the door when she came inside, or who had shown her how to trip the latch on the hidden key holder (a planter filled with a failing climbing rose) in case she found the door secured when she came home.

If the telephone rang in those hours before Julian came back from his office downtown, Anne answered it. So politely.

"Clarey residence," she would say, like a professional would. Like a visitor might. Mostly, it was one of my parents. Anne would say, "I'm sorry, my mom can't come to the phone right now."

My mother on the other line, something like: *Anne, honey, what's she doing right now?*

Then my daughter's voice, lower, the loud, airy whisper kids figure only the person they're talking to can hear, "Grandma, I don't know!"

Julian sent an old friend of ours around, Janine. I was glad when I looked through the peephole in the front door; I expected it was my mother on the porch again, but there was Janine, looking back at me through the convex glass, her lips pressed in and her eyes opened up a little expectantly.

I made her clear tea in my immaculate cups and we sat on the second-floor balcony off the master bedroom and shared cigarettes, though we both professed to have quit for good a decade ago.

"He's worried, you know," she told me.

I had known Janine years, for all of my adult life and a fair portion of my childhood. She had four children, three with her husband and a foster child named Blake, ten years old and scars across his back, and he was the same age as us when we'd become friends. He'd lived with them for nearly two years and still wouldn't talk about the scars. He'd stopped stealing money, stopped hoarding food, stopped wetting the bed, but wouldn't talk. They sent him to a child psychologist, who gave him Legos to play with and smelly markers with which to draw. The psychologist sent some of the drawings home with him, and brought Janine in to see what he'd built with the Legos: always houses with no windows and no doors.

I'd liked him, his deep green eyes and angry smile. I wished she'd brought him, but she'd come alone.

After a pause she said, "Julian is worried you might try to hurt yourself."

I looked at her.

Always people think this is the worst thing—that someone might try to die, but it's not. If you want to die maybe you still care a little bit. Maybe you think they'll all be sorry, or maybe you think of release. What it means is something still hurts, something *can* hurt. If you are past the point of dying, well, that's where the worry really is.

"I've been doing really well," I said. "Did you see the house when we came through? It's gorgeous."

"You're obsessing over it," she said. "He says you do nothing but clean and cook all day long. He says you virtually ignore Anne."

"I do not ignore her. We spend time in the afternoon. She helps me. And I do my best with her," I said. That was true. I looked at Janine, her slim hips and little high breasts, thick hair, brown bag hair. "I'm doing my best with everything."

"Well, that's what you can do, I guess."

"Thanks," I said.

"Your house *is* gorgeous. But your yard looks horrible," she said, teasing.

"I know." I'd lost hope for anything, the garden was so choked with weeds. Last year I had staked tomatoes and grown basil.

"I don't want to ask you anything you don't want to talk about," she said. "But we all wonder what's happening."

I thought of something I'd heard from a radio psychologist once—*Everything before* but *is bullshit*—and pulled on the long white cigarette.

"Laura?" Janine asked.

I looked at her again. My cigarette had burned all the way down.

"You've got to come back, okay?" she said.

"I'm right here," I said.

"I know you are. But you're somewhere else too."

I nodded.

"I miss you. You haven't come around in ages."

"I miss you too," I said, but I didn't know if I meant it. "I should start dinner."

"Julian said you've become a good cook. Maybe we can swap some recipes," she said, her pretty mouth turned up in a small smile. She wasn't silly enough to really suggest that we get out our index cards and trade. She was only trying—just like I was.

I stood up, held my arm over the railing of the balcony, and tossed the last of my cup of tea onto the ragged grass.

I liked to think that what I had was more than just your average case of middle-class ennui. Like I said, I'd been through therapy before and once I hit on this idea of grieving, of loss, I felt almost like I had a plan.

The day after Janine visited, before Anne was home from school and Julian from work, I went into the office. I used to spend a lot of time in that room, but lately it was Julian's place. He paid the bills and filed the receipts, he skulked around on the computer, working late. I sometimes went online to order things, but otherwise I ignored the business end of The Marriage.

I found some index cards, and I wrote out each part:

I deny that my finger is not injured.

I am angry that the threshold beyond the house is uncrossable.

I will bargain for the immunity of my daughter toward the situations of adults.

I am depressed about the garden.

I accept that my husband does not understand my predicaments.

I flipped through the five cards. They made about as much sense as anything else. I thought of maybe calling the school and telling them there was an emergency at home, but I was pretty sure that they wouldn't deliver Anne, and I would have to go pick her up, thus creating an actual emergency, the emergency of me behind the wheel. Not, it seemed, a good idea.

My next idea was to make a cocktail. Since this was something I could actually act on, I gathered up the index cards and went to the kitchen. I loved how the ice was so clear and how it snapped on the first pour of alcohol. I loved the glint of the clean glass against the smear of my fingerprints.

I read my cards again, I sipped my whiskey. It was too early to begin dinner, but too late to start any real project for the day. I wasn't really sure what I'd done with the morning, besides my five sentences.

I tried to think about how Julian might see me, or what he might do if he were me—he was always a good problem solver, but I think I didn't want to be solved. I only wanted my drink, my Anne, and the house. The house would keep me safe.

The Eggshells of Everything

It was October, so everything was dying from the garden to the yellow jackets, and while Mae loved the colors of the turned leaves and didn't mind the crispness in the air, she was restless watching the tomato vines go to rust and finding spent moths around the window casings. Wauconda, in rural eastern Washington, was small, almost not even a town. At the highway junction there was a gas station and restaurant that also had a postal counter.

Off the highway a few miles down was a simple, non-denominational church, and a few miles more down the pitted gravel road was the hall where monthly dances were held; it was in a field near the outdated one-room schoolhouse where she and her siblings attended lessons.

Her mother suggested the October dance—she was sixteen now, old enough to go on her own—and while Mae wasn't sure that watching a bunch of old farmers and ranchers stomp around to an awkwardly played fiddle would put her in better spirits, she knew the winter would mean a lot of nights cooped up at home, so she agreed.

Mae curled her hair and pinned it up, and swapped out her usual jeans for a clean skirt. Bruce, the youngest, drove her in the old truck—he was twelve and just learning. Mae could have walked or driven herself, but Bruce needed the practice. Mae held her tongue while he ground on the gears. *Clutch*, she thought, *clutch!* but she didn't say anything to him, because he was a lot better than her at that age. He'd had more experience, she figured, on the tractor, and she'd take house chores over dirty field work any day.

As they approached the hall, she saw first, before the outline of the building lit with string lights and before the dust settling, the silhouette of Frank, who had been two classes ahead of her before he left to go work in the mines. She hadn't put eyes on him in a year, but some people have a certain gait about them and she recognized him easily, and she was warm for a second in the cool autumn air. Mae got out of the truck and watched as Bruce clumsily tried to turn it around, the gears screeching.

Get! she thought at her brother, and she shifted from foot to foot, with one eye on him and one eye on her former schoolmate. Then the engine stalled and the truck was angled so it half-blocked the bumpy track that led up to the hall, and she heard the starter growling as Bruce cranked on it. When the engine engaged, he was flustered and he popped the clutch out too fast and the truck clunked again to a halt, smelling of gasoline and headlamps blazing.

"Hey, kid!" she heard Frank yell. "Kill the lights!"

Frank was laughing, holding a Mason jar. And his friends, who'd clearly been pulling from their own, were in a fit of giggles when Bruce switched into darkness.

Still, there was light enough from the dance to see Frank balance his jar on the hood of the car he had been leaning against and start off toward the truck, stumbling a little on the rough ground.

Mae heard her brother and Frank talking in low voices and a creaking that sounded like the clutch cable. Someone was hooting inside the hall and the band had started. A car approached down the single-lane road and flashed their lights.

"You can get around!" yelled Frank, and Mae heard the driver reply, *Hey! Frankie!* before the car lurched to the side to avoid Bruce and swing around to park.

"Ignore those assholes," she heard Frank say to Bruce as she came closer to them. Mae smiled. "Okay, make sure you're in first and then turn her over slow," Frank said.

Bruce worked at the ignition and the truck gurgled awake with a puff of oily exhaust.

"So, then, let out the clutch, little bit of gas, and when you feel that part at the top of the clutch where it catches, give it more gas," Frank said. "These old '27s are a bitch sometimes."

"C'mon, Bruce," she whispered. Mae saw Frank look over her brother's head and at her through the glaze of the passenger-side window. Then Bruce turned toward her as well, his face frozen in terror and shame. Maybe he wasn't so hot shifting the gears, but he was beyond needing such basic instructions. She smiled at her brother and gave him a small wave. His eyebrows came down some, he unpursed his lips, and he took his hand off the gearshift to wave back at Mae. *You're okay*, Mae thought.

Frank was still halfway up on the running board and leaning in the driver's side when Bruce pulled the lever for the lights, which came up fast and bright, and slipped his hand back onto the gearshift as he let the clutch out as smooth as a freshly ironed sheet. Frank hopped off and whooped at Mae's brother, who tooted the horn twice and disappeared down the dirt drive.

Mae waited for the bit of dust to settle after a few more drivers who'd been waiting ambled in to park, and she went toward Frank, who was back leaning against the hood of the car that held his open jar.

"Thank you," she said.

"Hello, girl," Frank said.

"Very nice instructions," she said.

"He's just a baby," Frank said. "He'll learn to handle that rig."

"He does all right," Mae said. She was the same height at sixteen as she had been the last time she'd seen him, but Frank had grown taller and full through the chest. She liked his slick of black hair and his battered boots.

"You going inside?" Frank asked as he pulled from his jar. He offered it to her.

"See you in there," said Mae, declining.

The hall was bright and the band was thumping. Mae reminded herself that she was only a twenty-minute walk from home if she decided she wanted to leave, just like walking home from school. Bruce would be around for her by eleven, but there was nothing keeping her if she didn't want to stay.

The county had been wet since the federal repeal of Prohibition almost twenty years prior, but the local preferences held on. The state liquor board ran a counter in town, but most of the drinkers were sipping from jars like Frank's, moonshine brewed in family stills. She didn't mind alcohol and had some on occasion, even if some people frowned on it for teenagers and women. Her mother said that nothing was wrong with drink, it was excess that was the problem, and Mae was inclined to believe this.

She scanned the hall, looking for someone she knew. She went to say hello to her mother's best friend, Eliza Svendsen, who kept one hand on her husband to steady him while she leaned in to hug Mae.

"Tell your mother I'm planning on coming around on Tuesday," Mrs. Svendsen said, still balancing the wobbly Mr. Svendsen.

"Yes, ma'am," Mae said. She could never call her Eliza, and she was in awe of what Mae thought of as a secret history. Mrs. Svendsen was part native, and her grandparents on her mother's side would have remembered a time before the peoples of Mr. Svendsen and her own parents took a claim on the ground. Mae loved how Mrs. Svendsen held something of this past—she worked as a midwife, knew the names of every plant, and refused to use the telephone.

There was punch set up on one side of the dance floor and Mae poured some and sniffed before she swallowed; it was heavy with the smell of booze and she wondered if Mr. Svendsen had been the one to doctor it or if he'd just had his fair share. She held her cup for a moment wondering if it was a good idea to take a drink, and decided to wait. She set the cup on the table and then she was above everything, the sawdust floor and the spiked punch and the Svendsens, twirling, her head high toward the rafters of the hall for a moment, her feet kicking against nothing but air.

"Still so tiny, Mae-fly," Frank said, as he set her down, carefully.

She realized then that he was very drunk, but she didn't care because his grip was steady and she hadn't been raised temperate. It was 1950, Mae thought; if she wanted to be flung around in the arms of a man, she was allowed to be.

One of the pins had come out of her hair and she felt the curls fall across her face. It was hot inside of the hall and she was sweating and damp at her neck. The band was a group of local boys and Mae had heard all the songs before, but there was something about the pace of the guitar and the look that Frank gave her and the way her head was still whirling from being spun above the dance floor that when he leaned down toward her and put his hand to her face and leaned in to kiss her, she let him, in public, in front of everyone.

By November the snow had come and when Mae dressed to visit the chicken coop on Sunday morning, her jeans and her collar felt snug. Maybe it was just too much salt, she thought; her mother was always warning her against salt, but Mae dashed it across her food anyway, enough so she could see the crystals glint in the yellow light hanging above the dinner table.

She scattered some handfuls of grain to draw the roosters away and then she reached her hands under the nesting hens. It always surprised Mae that they didn't peck at her when she dipped into their clutch. Her mother said that taking the eggs every day kept the girls laying, instead of getting broody. When they found the space beneath their bottoms empty, they just started over.

If this didn't make chickens one of the stupidest animals in the universe, Mae did not know what did.

She also checked around in the loose straw for stray eggs and when she found any, threw them against the side of the woodshed because it was too hard to track if these had been incubated. Her younger sister Eleanor, who at fourteen was between her and Bruce, never checked, and once Mae had opened a shell into the beginnings of a yellow cake and found a half chick inside. She had screamed at the sight of it, moldy feathers and a translucent, part-formed beak. Her mother scolded her for not mixing the yolks and whites together in a separate bowl before adding them to the batter, which was ruined now, and slopped the raw cake into the yard where the dog licked it up, chick and all, and then vomited from all the sugar an hour later.

Mae was tired and the ammonia smell of the chicken shit was making her light-headed. She would remind Bruce that it was his turn to clean the coop. The night before, Mae had turned in early, but she was restless. Her bed felt lumpy and her pillow either too fluffed or too flat, and the bedroom she shared with Eleanor was cold and noisy. The noise she blamed on Eleanor's snores and she cursed her sister in the bottom bunk, sleeping peacefully through the night.

She took her basket inside, orbs of green and brown spotted with dung, and washed all of them under the cool tap. There was another basket they kept in the refrigerator, and she counted out enough eggs for breakfast before putting the new eggs in to keep cold. She hung the collecting basket on the hook by the doorway.

Mae washed her hands and then started making biscuits with lard, flour, and buttermilk. She added a pinch of soda and she got the pin from the cupboard and floured it along with the cutter, making perfect rounds that she placed one by one onto a baking sheet slick from use out of a smaller and smaller flat of dough until there was one piece left which she shaped with her hands.

The house they lived in had always had basic electricity— lights and power for the pump to the well, but in recent years her father had talked her mother into getting the wiring done for a proper refrigerator and a range. Her mother hadn't seen the point. With three children, the food was gone before the block in the icebox melted anyway, and they had to chop wood for heat, so what was a little more to bake with. In the end her father had won this argument and now the old wood cooker was out in his workshop, though if they had a big gathering around the holidays, her mother would clean it out and use it for a bird, since she thought the flavor was better. The icebox was in the workshop too, holding cans of paint and solvents and other bits of chemical leftovers that her mother didn't think should be stored in the open. They still used the outdoor toilet—her parents both thought that water was too precious to flush with—which Mae didn't mind.

She focused on breakfast. She put the biggest cast-iron pan they had on the largest coil burner on the range and dropped in a tablespoon of bacon grease to heat so she could fry the eggs while her biscuits were cooking. She would make two for everyone except herself, even though she was very, very hungry. The night before, as Mae and Eleanor were doing up the dinner dishes, their mother had come into the kitchen and sent Eleanor out of the room. Mae watched her little sister go, and she put her rag down. It was very hard for Mae to keep her face straight as she listened to her mother, even though she tried to clench her jaw into what looked like some casual version of *Oh, you don't say?* Her hands were raw from the hot water and her teeth were grinding.

"You've been eating a lot and you've been at the outhouse all day," her mother had said. "Anything you want to tell me?"

"No," Mae said. She had brown hair and weighted ninety-two pounds. She had never had much appetite, but starting a few weeks after the dance she'd had a knot in her stomach and the only thing that would soothe it was food.

Her mother had left the kitchen and sent Eleanor back in to finish the drying, and Mae felt suddenly the urge to urinate, but she was not sure if it was only because her mother had mentioned it, and in any case, she clenched her legs.

As the bacon fat started to warm for breakfast, she thought it smelled rancid. She checked the tin twice and there was nothing wrong with it, so she cracked nine eggs into the pan as soon as it started to really sizzle.

She had the coffee boiling and breakfast was almost ready when she heard her father come in from the barn with her brother. Her mother and sister wandered into to the kitchen to set the table. Usually they all served themselves, but Mae told them all to sit and she slid the eggs—perfectly how her father liked them, firm whites, wobbly yolk—onto their plates, put the pan on a trivet to cool, and passed around the biscuits. She'd already taken some butter out of the fridge and let it sit on the stove to get soft, and her sister had put out honey and jam.

"No meat?" her brother asked.

"You mean, *Thank you, Mae,*" her mother said.

"Thank you, Mae," her brother said.

"Thank you, Mae," her father said.

She wished she had made another egg for herself.

She saw Eleanor go for a second biscuit piled with a spoonful of jam and dab of the partly melted butter and she felt very angry. She felt sick from cooking and the chickens but starving at the same time, but she ate only her single egg and a biscuit top, dry.

After the breakfast dishes, Mae lingered in the kitchen, wiping at the already clean countertops and straightening up the cabinets and reorganizing the silverware drawer so that every fork and every spoon was stacked perfectly against the curve of the one below.

She worked on her schoolwork at the kitchen table. It was very hard to concentrate. The kitchen still smelled like pork fat and even though she'd washed up everything very carefully she would have sworn that there was still a bit of burned egg and burned biscuit on the corners of the pans, and she wanted to relieve herself but felt sure her mother was watching for her.

She was supposed to be doing figures. She'd always liked the neatness of math and liked school in general, but most of the other upper-school girls had already left to get married, and there was only one boy her age left, Neil, who she didn't care for. If Neil wasn't the human being closest in the world to a chicken, she didn't know who was. College was out of the question but both her mother and her father wanted her to finish high school at least, but she wasn't so sure. Some of the older boys Mae knew had gone to the Korean War. She couldn't imagine it. She already wondered if she was getting too old to find a husband, and now there was this issue of her snug jeans, her hunger.

Mae finished a column of division, which had taken her longer than it ought to have. In a month, she hadn't stopped thinking about the kiss between her and Frank, though she had finally decided that she didn't regret it. She thought as the night went on, though, she shouldn't have let him go so far.

November was dragging on. It would be Thanksgiving soon, and Mae hoped that Frank would come down from the mines for the holiday, and she hoped that he would call at the house. Their fathers knew one another. The least he could do was come for a hello, she thought. They weren't the type of families that required formal courting, but she was starting to worry.

At school, she did something that she'd never done before and would have slapped someone else for doing: she stole half of one of the younger kid's lunches because she was so, so hungry. She snuck off for just a minute at the noon hour with a piece of ham and a hard-boiled egg and devoured it with her own biscuit and cheese, and she hardened her face when she returned to the schoolhouse and saw Celia still crying at having opened her pail to only a piece of greasy bread and a mealy apple. Mae went to find her brother and her sister with her secret, full stomach and made them divide up their lunches so the younger girl would have at least something decent, and when the teacher asked her what had happened, Mae said that part of Celia's food had a bad smell and the teacher thanked Mae for watching out for the little children.

Mae went back to her desk and put her hand on her belly.

Is this how you will make me be? she asked, and she resolved to talk to her mother.

She felt already the child was a boy; she felt already she would not name him for Frank.

They did the clothes washing in the side room, a partly enclosed porch that was sweltering in the summer and freezing in the winter. Mae wished they would get an electric washer, but, for now, there was no appliance forthcoming. Long ago her father had installed a brick pit to heat water, and Mae and her mother doubled up, her mother stirring the coals and Mae keeping watch on the electric burners in the kitchen.

Mae had been wondering through several loads of sheets and a batch of her father's barn clothes how to open the conversation.

When she finally started it all came pouring out of her, backward: the hunger; the smell of the grease tin; the sips she'd finally taken from the mason jar that had helped her tolerate his soft, sour breath until he convinced her to lay with him as if they were married; the way she'd felt when Frank held her high above the dance floor.

"Frankie Collins?" her mother asked.

"Yes, ma'am," Mae said.

"Better than a stranger," her mother said.

Mae wasn't sure if she agreed, and she gouged at some dish towels in the laundry pot, looking for stains.

Her mother wanted to know how long it had been. Mae was sorry, then, that she hadn't come to her sooner.

"I think we are late," Mae's mother said. "Eliza may know some cures."

"Don't tell Mrs. Svendsen," said Mae. "Pennyroyal only works on cows."

"She'll find out soon enough. And there are some others—nutmeg, tansy, oranges. Actually, I am not sure how the orange cure works, but these are only for very early pregnancies. I don't want you to get sick."

Mae sat down and watched the laundry reach a boil. "I'm too young," she said.

"I know," her mother said. "But it's happening now."

This year their Thanksgiving table would be small. Mae's grandparents on both sides had passed, and her father's brother had moved to Oregon. Mae's mother's sisters were scattered across the Northwest as well. This year it would be just them and the Svendsens, who didn't want to travel to Seattle where Clive Svendsen's family lived.

Mae's mother asked her to come into the kitchen. Though Eliza had no children, her mother's friend had a reputation as one of the best midwives in the county. They had talked it over, and decided that they would not try any herbs. Mrs. Svendsen knew the citrus cure, but she didn't think it was safe.

"Maybe we will put some medicine on Frankie Collins," she said.

"Please, no," Mae begged.

"Has he come for you in these days?" Mae's mother asked.

"No," said Mae. Her stomach turned.

"Then he takes his medicine," said Mrs. Svendsen.

At the table that afternoon, Mae's mother led the blessing, listing all of the usual things. As she always did when Mrs.

Svendsen was present, she deferred to a general creator, not Jesus. "And," she said, "we give thanks for the souls of those who are among us but who we do not know yet."

"Dig in," her father said, closing in the way that was his tradition.

Mae felt her insides gurgle, and she made it halfway across the yard on her way to the outhouse before she had to stop to be sick, kneeling there in front of the kitchen window. When she was done, she kicked snow over her vomit the way a cat would and stood outside, her body hot and steaming in the cold.

Her mother was not happy with Mae's situation, but she was kind. Mae still had the chicken chores and breakfast; she still helped with the laundry. But her mother told her father and her mother told her siblings. They had been raised around animals so there was nothing to explain. Bruce said he was sorry that he was late in picking her up from the dance, because he had fallen asleep in the hayloft listening to the radio.

"You couldn't have changed it," she told him, and she knew she would always remember him in the moment when she smiled at him and his face turned from mortified to confident and he navigated expertly away from her.

She wondered if it would be the same with her own child.

Her weight crept up; for the first time in her life, Mae was over one hundred pounds. Her father said she was still only two bales of good hay; any man worth a day in the field could lift her easily, a thousand times. Eleanor still snored at night, but if Mae woke her on trips to the outhouse she'd whisper in the dark: *Sister, can I bring you anything? Water? Beef jerky?*

Her parents and her siblings showed her how special it was to bear a child, how sacred.

The school did not feel the same way. Even before the winter holidays, the baby of Frank was starting to show. She tried wearing her mother's clothing, which was large and baggy on her, but even with the extra weight, Mae was so tiny that there was nowhere to hide.

Her teacher sent her home one day at the noon hour. The snow had been falling heavily since morning.

"Go," her teacher said. "And pray to God this child's father marries you."

"I'd like to complete the term," Mae said. Frank had still not come for her, and it felt like her parents were right that she should finish school.

"You cannot," said her teacher.

"I can be an example to the younger girls," Mae said.

"I don't need a bad example in my school," said the teacher.

Mae's lunch pail had been overflowing—*eat*, said her mother, *eat*—so she emptied her slices of ham and bread, boiled eggs, and walnuts on Celia's desk, buttoned her coat, and started walking. When she looked behind her toward the school, she saw Eleanor and Bruce running after her, Eleanor struggling in a pair of heavy boots, and Bruce, though he was younger, pulling her along. Mae stopped and waited for them, and then they all three made their way in the new drifts.

They lived in a beautiful place, Mae thought as they walked, surrounded by the tall, quiet pines and icy creeks. The sky was streaked with white and when she looked back at the school again, the woodsmoke piping from the chimney smudged the horizon and the gentle wind had already mostly covered their tracks in the fine snow. They passed the hall, which looked pretty with icicles coming off the eaves, and headed toward the main road that would take them home.

When Frank had taken her to the back of his friend's car, he smelled like hooch and grease gravy, and though he was not her first, she let him believe that he was because she thought anyone who could willingly go down in a mine every day must be sold on searching for something special.

The wind was picking up and the snow falling harder, but her brother's and sister's hands laced in hers on either side and her growing belly kept her warm.

There is no god, she said back to her teacher in her head, clenching her siblings' fingers through their homemade mittens, *only family*.

WENDY J. FOX holds an MFA from the Inland Northwest Center for Writers and has contributed to literary journals including *Washington Square*, *The Missouri Review* (online), *The Madison Review*, *PMS poemmemoirstory*, *The Tusculum Review* and *ZYZZVA*. Her nonfiction was included in *Tales from the Expat Harem: Foreign Women in Modern Turkey* (Seal Press), a #1 English-language bestseller which was recommended by *National Geographic Traveler* and featured on *The Today Show*. In 2011, she was selected for Dzanc Books' Emerging Writers Network short-story month. This year, she will attend Bread Loaf. In her day job, she is the director of marketing for a technology company. *The Seven Stages of Anger* is her debut collection of stories, and is the first winner of the Press 53 Award for Short Fiction.

Cover artist STACY ANN YOUNG has been creating art for over twenty-five years, which has evolved from colored pencil to her current medium of digital creations, blending photography with digital manipulation and photo blending. She lives near Portland, Oregon, in the ever-inspiring Pacific Northwest and is currently working on a number of exciting art projects.

CPSIA information can be obtained
at www.ICGtesting.com
Printed in the USA
FFOW05n1918021014